AUTUMN AT THE WILLOW RIVER GUESTHOUSE

CP WARD

AUTUMN AT THE WILLOW RIVER GUESTHOUSE

1

BREAKDOWN

THEY CALLED IT THE RAT RACE, BUT IT WAS MORE LIKE
the robot race, Lily Markham thought, as she resisted the
urge to thump the horn one more futile time. She was
penned in on all sides by traffic, surrounded by a sea of
belching, rumbling metal. Through tinted windows she
glimpsed other drivers, some appearing as frustrated as
she, others less so, their phones in their hands, one rifling
through a rucksack, another with a razor pressed against
his chin.

Lily had left her phone at home, and just yesterday she
had finished the book she always kept in the car, forgetting
to replace it with another from the pile of recent impulse
buys she kept on the table in the hall. It was still in the
glove box, and she supposed she could read it again, if she
really had to.

If she really wasn't destined to get to work on
time today.

But as always, like the giant, creeping behemoth that
London's traffic was, eventually she did start to move,

slipping the car into drive, inching forward a few more metres, before coming to a halt again.

Perhaps this morning it was something interesting, rather than the usual boringness of rush hour. Perhaps there was a climate change protest going on, and some hippies had glued themselves to the road. Maybe a farmer had got lost and brought a herd of cattle into the city centre. Or maybe some idiot had simply run out of petrol.

She glanced at her own gauge. Half full. No problem.

The car in front inched forward again, and Lily pulled the lever down into drive.

Something clicked behind the dashboard, and suddenly the lever took on an unfamiliar looseness, floppy and useless like a broken ruler.

Oh please no.

Lily gave it a frantic tug, but it was no use.

She closed her eyes, for a moment wishing the whole world would just disappear. At least if she opened her eyes again to a black void, she would escape the irrefutable embarrassment that was heading her way like a thundering ghost train.

Then, inevitably, she opened them again, to find someone peering in at her window and then pointing at the stretch of open road in front of her.

'Miss, could you get a move on, please?' came a muffled voice through the window. 'Some of us are trying to get to work.'

'So what did you do in the end? Call the AA?'

'The police showed up before the AA could even get close. They were directing traffic and everything. I wanted to die. Melissa from next door told me it made the lunchtime news.'

'Oh. Well, I suppose fame is fame, isn't it?' Lily's mother, Sarah Markham, chuckled. 'Did you get a raise?'

'A raise? I almost got fired. I missed a meeting with an important financier. According to Jonas, he had a bit of a tantrum about it, and we might end up missing out on a half million-pound contract.'

'That's too bad.'

Lily peered at her face in the mirror across the hall. Curtains of mahogany brown hair encircled an oval face that looked gaunter by the day. Steve still told her she was beautiful. She wished he'd stop lying to her and tell the truth.

Replace the posh woolly thing from Topshop with a pointed hat and switch out your Laura Evans jacket for a grey-green robe and you could start putting spells on people.

She shook her head. 'I'm tired, Mum. I need a holiday.'

'Well, we're always ready for you. Ah, here's your dad. I'll put him on a minute. I've got a casserole overboiling.'

There was a click as the phone was put down, then a moment later Lily's dad came on the line.

'Hey sweetheart. I hear you're having a bad day.'

Lily couldn't help but smile. While Sarah could be a little spiky even on a good day, Pete Markham had a voice that naturally soothed her. The voice that had read her bedtime stories for years just had something about it that made her feel safe.

'Mum managed to relay that pretty quick,' she said.

'It's a father's natural instinct,' Pete said. 'Plus, it's Wednesday. You always call on either a Monday or a Saturday. You haven't called on a Wednesday since you had that water pipe burst last January.'

'You remember that?'

Pete chuckled. 'I remember my little girl being upset.'

Lily sighed. She had always been a Daddy's girl. She had pretended to be dyslexic for two years in order to keep their story time together. She had only been forced to admit that she could read perfectly well when her mother had started to suggest a special school.

'I'll be all right,' Lily said, trying to sound better than she felt. She stared at herself in the mirror again, struggling to see a twenty-six-year-old staring back. 'How's the van?'

'It was a good summer,' Pete said. 'I sold out almost every day. Thinking of getting some kind of pumpkin hot dog thing going on for the autumn, though. Be a bit seasonal, and all that.'

'Good luck. Save one for me.'

'Will you get down for a visit?'

'I don't know. I mean, I'm flat out with work, even when the car's running. And then of course, there's the wedding....'

'Ah, yes. Any more news on that?'

Finally, Lily had cause to smile. She thought of Steve, the way he'd gone down on one knee, and her heart felt all squishy inside. The look in his eyes ... the way the sun had glittered off the ring as he held it up ... she'd dreamed of that moment since she was a little girl. She hadn't expected it to come in the middle of a day out at London Zoo, but Steve claimed flamingoes were a symbol of love, so who was she to complain?

'We're both so busy with work, but probably it won't happen until the spring. Steve wants something big, loads of people, all that. He said he's only going to do it once, of course.'

'Let's hope so.'

On the tabletop, Lily's work phone began to buzz. She looked at it, recognising Jonas's number.

'Dad, I'd better go.'

'Okay, dear. Just remember, whatever happens, we're here for you. And currently so's your old room, although your mother's keen to turn it into some kind of craft space. She wants an art room, I want a wine store.' Pete chuckled. 'We'll let you have the deciding vote. Don't forget how I always used to pump up your bike tyres and lie to your mother about you peeing in the bath?'

'Dad!'

'Speak to you soon, sweetheart.'

She said goodbye and hung up. Usually talking to Dad —and even talking to Mum—cheered her up, but the little icon flashing on her work phone was like a stone poking into her back. It was nearly nine. Jonas wasn't above out of hours contact, but by nine he was usually in a wine bar wooing some potential new client or running one of his endless late-night marathons that he insisted on telling everyone about.

She picked up the phone, her hand shaking, and pressed **OPEN**.

My office on Floor 13, 9 a.m. tomorrow morning. For once, don't be late.

2

THIRTEENTH FLOOR

Jonas, I'm sorry, it was beyond my control. It was a freak problem. It'll never happen again.

Lily repeated her apology like a mantra as the lift bore her up to the thirteenth and last floor of Davidson Tower. As the lights rose one by one, Lily stared at the plaque next to the control panel, one whose contents she had stared at a thousand times over the last four years, the bold proclamation burned into the back of her skull.

Built in 1967, Davidson Tower is the home of Davidson Financial Services, founded by Sir Richard Davidson of Norfolk, United Kingdom. Founded by a man who made his own luck from the day he came kicking and screaming into the world, Davidson Financial Services has been a world leader in loans and finances for more than fifty years. "Countries kneel at the hand of war but pray at the altar of finance."

There was no mention of the thirteenth floor, but like Orwell's Room 101, within the company it was legendary. Sir Richard had built the tower with thirteen floors in order to challenge fate itself, then built all the executive suites and offices there for the same reason, to laugh in the face of luck. Rather contradictorily, however, all the meeting rooms where negotiations took place were on Floor 7.

From the lift, Jonas Davidson's office was at the end of the corridor, the wall and door that blocked her view the only part of Floor 13 that didn't appear to be made of glass. Lily gave a polite knock, then entered on command into a vertigo-inducing office in which there seemed to be no back wall, just an open space that looked out over London. It was an impressive view, for sure, but in a place where the edge of carpet had a little downturn before it touched the glass to give the illusion that it was falling away into nothing, she wondered how it was possible to concentrate.

Jonas sat behind his desk, as usual on a call. He waved at her to sit on a sofa by the inside wall, as though he was about to give her a therapy session. Time management, perhaps, or how to know in advance whether a car has a freak fault or not. While she waited, she studied her boss and the company CEO. He looked pretty much how CEOs did on TV, handsome in a sunbed, possibly-surgically altered kind of way, but with an inwards tilt to his eyebrows and a hard set to his mouth that meant even when he was laughing he never looked truly happy. For some reason, with the cobalt grey of his suit, he reminded her of a rogue submarine, hunting through the seas for ships to torpedo without warning.

He put down the phone and glanced at his watch. 'Well, there's a first time for everything.' Then, clicking his fingers at her as though she were some kind of dog, he pointed at the chair across from his desk and said, 'You may advance.'

Lily took this to mean that she should leave the relative comfort of the sofa and sit directly across from him on the firing chair, which had sweat stains on the armrests from all the other employees who had made it their final destination on the way out of the company. At least, that was how the legend went.

'You wanted to see me, sir?'

Jonas just started at her. 'You're from Devon, are you not?'

Lily nodded. Jonas could know every detail about her just by looking at his computer screen, but this was all part of the game.

'Yes. Willow River.'

'That's a town name?'

She nodded. 'Well, more of a village. It only has about thirty houses. It's just outside of Brentwell—'

'That's nice.' Jonas leaned forward. 'I've never willingly been to the countryside. I don't like all the chitchat and the coffee mornings and the sitting around in parks. I find such trivial things a waste of time.'

'Oh. That's a shame.'

'My father built this tower,' Jonas said. 'Do you know how many trees he had destroyed in order to break ground?'

Lily smiled. 'I don't, but if you told me the square metreage of the site, I could make an educated guess.'

Jonas nodded. 'Educated. There's another relevant word. You were the best in your class. Oxford, wasn't it?'

'Yes. Economics.'

'You have all the goods, Lillian. You have the education, the smarts, you're even beautiful—'

Lily gave another awkward smile, wondering if it was her turn to be the subject of one of Jonas's legendary advances. She had so far avoided it, but her engagement to Steve was now common knowledge and Jonas might view that as a challenge.

'—although I would suggest finding a more upmarket hair stylist before your wedding day.'

Lily's smile dropped.

'What you can't seem to shake loose from is your heritage.'

'My—'

'You country folk, you just can't adapt to city life. You can't just amble along, pushing your wheelbarrow, leading your horse and cart, stopping to complain about the weather with Mabel or Earnest or whatever worryingly-back-in-vogue names all you country lot have.' He punched a fist into a palm. 'You have to have the drive—and I'm not talking about cars, here, although I understand that's another of your shortcomings—and you have to have the nerve to get things done. Do you know how much money we didn't make yesterday due to your tardiness?'

Lily looked down. He was getting to the point now. 'About half a million pounds?'

'Nearly three quarters!' Jonas said. 'Do you know what we can buy with three quarters of a million pounds?'

'A chateau in France?'

'Stock! More and more stock! With careful management, that three quarters of a million could have been two million by the end of next week, had it not been for your inability to get to work on time. And not only that, but are you aware that you made the BBC News?'

'Someone downstairs mentioned it—'

'As a result, our own stock price dropped by almost a twentieth of a percent. Do you know how much money that is?'

Lily grimaced. 'Honestly, I have no idea.'

'It's due to this lack of consideration for what's around you that I've had to come to this decision, Lillian. I like you. You have everything to succeed in financial management except the most important thing: city smarts. I don't want to let you go, but I have no choice. Do you know how many applicants we had for your job?'

'No.'

'All of them.' Jonas clicked his fingers again and pointed at the door. 'Thank you for your efforts, Lillian. Collect your things on the way out. HR will arrange a decent severance, so there won't be any reason for you to bother suing us.'

Lily stood up. Her shoulders felt weak, her head too heavy. She shuffled towards the door, face smarting. The smug tycoon with his suit that cost the same as ten African villages set in motion a little roller ball ornament, then chuckled as he put a finger in between the swinging chrome balls to disrupt their clicking harmony.

There wasn't a single colour in the room that wasn't a shade of black or metallic grey. Lily paused by the door and looked back.

'You know, sir, what would look nice in here?'

'What?'

'A house plant or two.'

Jonas chuckled. 'Plants don't grow fast enough for my liking,' he said. 'Not like investments. That's real life, right there. Do I need to call security?'

Lily shook her head. 'No. I'm going.'

The lift took her back down. She stared at the plaque by the controls, wanting to rip it off the wall, but certain that it was either fitted too tight, or alarmed. The Davidson financial empire took no chances.

It took her only a few minutes to collect her things. As she packed away her personal items—a photo of her family taken on a camping trip in Cornwall a few years ago, a little pink pig toy her nephew had given her for her last birthday, and a small ceramic house she had bought in Quimbeck in the Lake District on a trip with her university friends—she could only frown at how little actual stuff she had used in her job. Davidson Financial Services was a paperless company, and only the shiny laptop on her desk remained behind. Remembering the work phone, she took it out of her pocket and set it down on top of the closed laptop. Then, she looked up and around to see if anyone had noticed her departure.

An engineer was standing by the coffee machine, the control panel open. A couple of other consultants were standing nearby, looking frustrated, but otherwise, all heads were down, the cubicle walls cutting off any possibility of contact.

Buried in her work, this sanitised, soulless place had been her home from home the last four years. In a moment it had been pulled out from under her.

Lily gulped. Then, without warning, the tears began to come. She stood there, her hands in her pockets, one hand encircling the toy pig, the other the ceramic house, tears streaming down her cheeks. No one looked up, no one said a word.

After a couple of minutes, the sobbing stopped. As anonymously as she had worked, Lily headed for the exit, wondering what on earth she was going to do now.

3
____

REJECTION

'Where are you?'

'I'm at a café on Holder Street. Finchley's. Can you come and meet me?'

'Aren't you supposed to be at work?'

'That's just it. I got fired. My car broke down yesterday, and I missed an important meeting.'

The other end of the line went quiet for a few seconds. Steve was on the Underground, and Lily hoped he had gone into a tunnel.

'Oh, well, I suppose that could be a problem,' he said at last.

'I got a decent pay off,' Lily said. 'And they gave me a reference, which was a surprise. I'm not going to starve.' She smiled. The sacking still hurt, but she was trying to look on the bright side, something her dad had always taught her.

Life could always get worse.

'And … we could even see each other more. I could come around to the studio and watch you work.'

Again, a long pause. Another tunnel perhaps. The Underground really needed to put a few signal masts in.

'Well, I mean, you could. That would be great.'

'I wouldn't get in the way—'

'But I do need silence when I work.'

'You're always playing music.'

'That gets me in the zone. So, does this mean I'm going to have to put in a government grant application? You are going to look for another job, aren't you?'

'Well, of course.'

'Phew. So I can hold off the application for now?'

Lily shrugged. 'Well, I suppose so. We can talk more about it when you get here.'

'Okay. I shouldn't be long.'

Putting her own timekeeping troubles to shame, Lily was on her third coffee by the time Steve finally showed up. As he walked into Finchley's, he held up two carrier bags from the art shop up the road and shrugged.

'Sorry, I just couldn't resist. You know what us artists are like. Shall I get you another coffee?'

'I'll have an orange juice. Otherwise I don't think I'll sleep tonight.'

Steve dropped his goods down on the chair across from Lily and went to order the drinks. Lily glanced into the bag. A few packs of paint brushes and some oil paints. She gave an uneasy smile. He had gone for the expensive brands again. Perhaps now she was unemployed, she ought to ask for her credit card back. They would certainly have to talk about a little downsizing, at least until she could get another job.

Steve came back over. He set the drinks down, then

leaned over and kissed her cheek before sitting down opposite. 'So, all that country timing caught up with you, did it? Isn't that what he called it last time?'

Lily sighed. 'You know, I had a look back at my diary. It was only the third time in the last year. Once was due to a bus driver's strike. Admittedly the other was when I overslept after you switched off my alarm—'

'I don't think blaming me will solve anything.'

'I'm not blaming you. It's just a fact. And the third was yesterday. A little harsh, don't you think?'

Steve shrugged. 'Perhaps it was just an excuse. How much did you get in severance?'

'Six months.'

Steve nodded. 'Well, that's pretty good. And if you get a new job soon, you can double down. Maybe I can afford a bigger studio—'

'I was thinking of taking a couple of months off.'

Steve frowned. 'Why?'

Lily shook her head. 'I don't know, perhaps because for the last four years I've worked roughly seventy hours a week and haven't taken a single holiday in all that time.'

'Yeah, but what would you do?'

'Maybe I could do an art course or something. Perhaps you could teach me.'

Steve suppressed a sigh. 'I'm pretty busy with the new project. Look, I have an idea. Why don't we go away for the weekend? You know, book a posh place in the Lake District or something, somewhere inspiring. After that, you'll feel better.' He leaned over and patted her hand. 'I know job hunting is hard. You might have to downsize a little, but with Davidson's on your resume, you'll get something easily.'

'But maybe I want to take a break.'

Steve let go of her hand and sat back. 'Are you really

thinking about this clearly? This is London. You can't just sit around unemployed. You have rent to pay. And what about me?'

Lily bit her tongue. She didn't want to say it, because she knew they would have an argument, and right now she wanted nothing less. But the words gnawed at her like a rat biting her shoe.

'Perhaps you could sell some of your work?'

Steve stared at her. 'So you're making this about money now, are you? I'm an artist, Lily. It's not about money.'

'It is when it's about mine.'

Steve rolled his eyes, then looked from side to side while giving a fishlike pout. Lily had always found him so handsome, but she hated it when he did this. It took twenty years off him, regressing him into a petulant twelve-year-old who had found cress sandwiches in his school lunch instead of tuna-mayo.

'So you think I'm sponging off you, do you? I can't believe you'd accuse me of something like that.'

'Steve—'

He pushed back his chair and stood up. Then, almost as an afterthought, he picked up the bags of art supplies and waved them in front of him. 'I'll take this back. Right now. Will that make you happy?'

'You don't have to—'

'It will, won't it? It's always been about money with you.'

Before Lily could say anything else, Steve had turned and stormed out, the bell over Finchley's door giving an angry little rattle as the door bumped shut behind him. Lily stared at the door, trying not to cry, then gathered her things together and made to leave, but not before visiting the toilet. After all, she had drunk three large coffees while waiting for Steve, and now that she was stuck with buses while her car was being repaired, she didn't know when she might get another chance.

Conveniently, it had begun to rain. The hot August afternoon seemed to steam as the rain came down, leaving Lily both wet and sweaty. Halfway to the bus stop, she gave up and just ducked into the nearest pub.

At two in the afternoon, it was almost empty. A couple of suits with their ties loosened were playing pool, while a greybeard in an anorak was sitting at the bar, sipping a pint while watching horse racing on a television hung from the ceiling.

'What can I get you?' a woman behind the bar asked.

'A Manhattan.'

'A what?'

'It's a cocktail.'

The woman smiled. 'The Ritz is a couple of stops up the Tube. This is a pub, dear. If you tell me what to put in it, I'll have a decent go, but if you want cherries and fancy umbrellas and all that, you'll have to nip up to the Tesco Metro.' She grinned. 'I'll hold your stool.'

Lily looked around at the lines of beer taps and spirits. 'You do have a toilet, don't you?' she asked the woman.

'This is a pub, dear, so yes.'

Lily smiled. 'In that case, I'll have a pint.'

4

EVICTION

You could take the bumpkin out of the countryside, but not the countryside out of the bumpkin, Lily reasoned, as she half stumbled, half skipped up the road from the bus stop. After a few uneasy moments getting off the bus, she was feeling a little more confident now that she recognised the park just down the street from her flat. The cones and ticker-taped fence surrounding a section of crumbling pavement was still there, as was Old Len, the local tramp, sitting on the bench outside the park. The new sky blue Merc that someone down the street owned was still there, now parked in the same spot where she had always parked. It didn't matter. She didn't care.

She had lost a lot of money over the last couple of hours, but regained a little of her enjoyment of life. Gary, the greybeard, had turned out to be an even worse pool player than she, fluffing a final black chance to beat Jim and Phillip, the two account managers skiving off from Lloyds TSB for the afternoon. Thrilled with their victory, Lily had bought the tequilas in but turned down the offer of an early trip to a club, waving them off as they swayed

"

up the street, the lads on either side with Gary in the middle, an arm round the shoulder of each. Feeling a general anger over her life, she had given them all the cash out of her wallet—just over two hundred pounds—then frustratingly realised she needed to find a cashpoint in order to pay for a bus ticket. Deciding instead to be a total rebel, she had decided to jump the bus, before having an abrupt change of heart and offering the driver her watch in lieu of payment.

Lindsay, her downstairs neighbour, was standing outside on the street, her two young boys tucked under her arms. Lily stopped beside her, frowning at the suitcases lined up on the pavement.

'Alright, you. Looks like you've had a fun afternoon,' Lindsay said, as her two boys, Stan and Rick, chimed in with twin 'Alrights'.

'I had the afternoon off,' Lily said, trying not to slur. 'What's going on? Are you off on holiday?'

'Chance would be a fine thing. Didn't they call you?'

'Who?'

'The council. We've been shut down. Waiting for my mum to pick us up. Something about fire regs.'

'What?'

'They called me at work.'

Lily pulled out her phone. She had turned it off after meeting Steve, but now she found five missed calls from an unknown number.

'They were doing some work on the place next door,' Lindsay said. 'Found something off, so the geezer from the council said. There he is now, if you want to have a word. I imagine he'll let you go in and pick up some bits if you need to.'

Lily was fast sobering up. She stared as the door to her building opened and a council worker wearing a white helmet and a bright orange vest came down the front steps.

'Ah, here's Mum,' Lindsay said, as a black Volvo pulled up to the curb. 'Hopefully it'll only be a few weeks. We'll have to have coffee.'

Unable to find the strength to speak, Lily stared dumbly as Lindsay loaded the boys and their cases into the car, then waved as it pulled away. She stood gaping on the curb for another minute until the council worker, who had busied himself rearranging a line of cones across two parking spaces she assumed would be for council vehicles, came wandering over.

'Are you Miss Markham? Flat Four?'

'Uh.' Lily nodded.

'You weren't answering the phone. I'm afraid a serious breach of safety regulations has been discovered, so we've had to clear you all out while we sort it. Should only be a few weeks.' He reached into his pocket and pulled out a little booklet of what looked like coupons. 'These are for the City Lodge up the street. And you'll be compensated, don't worry.'

Lily stared at him. 'I don't need money,' she muttered. 'I need a soul.'

'Have you tried the Tesco Metro up on St John's Road?'

'Huh?' Lily shook her head.

'Listen, I'm about to go and get sausage and chips, but I can hang on five minutes if you want to go inside and get some stuff. Don't worry about any kind of contamination. Anything you leave behind will be safe.' He clapped his hands together and grinned. 'A bit like a free holiday, isn't it? I heard they have a great buffet breakfast up at the City Lodge.'

'Breakfast....'

'Yeah, you can get your usual cornflakes or whatever but they've got all this weird foreign stuff too, like bagels and things.'

Lily just nodded. 'I'll just be five minutes,' she said, but when she tried to step out into the road, her feet wouldn't move. She still had her hands in her pockets, and she squeezed the little pig for comfort, trying not to cry.

'Are you all right about all this?' the council worker said.

Lily gave a dumb shake of her head.

'I imagine it must come as a bit of a shock.' He chuckled. 'It did to us too. I know it's an inconvenience, but it won't be for long. If the City Lodge isn't up to your liking, perhaps you could go and stay with some family or something?'

Lily tried to muster the strength to reply, but all she really wanted right now was to sleep. Finally she managed to force her feet to move, taking her across the street, into the narrow entrance and up the stairs to her second floor flat. Number four of six on three floors, she had lived here since graduating from university, paying the expensive deposit with her first salary from Davidson's.

She had thought she was happy. The advertisement listed it as a three-room studio apartment, but now that she looked at it, she realised it was a glorified bedsit. Her bed was tucked in behind a sofa that faced a rented TV she could have just bought straight out, but had by now paid two or three times over its face value. The little kitchenette was connected by a couple of paces to where she slept, and one of the three "rooms" was the bathroom. The other she guessed had to be the hall or a walk-in closet beside the front door.

Her one suitcase sat inside, half concealed by several expensive coats. She chose one just in case it got chilly later, then quickly filled the suitcase with her belongings. To her surprise and no little worry, almost everything she actually owned fitted neatly inside. She had never really gone crazy with clothes, and most of her other "stuff" was electronic: a laptop, a phone, and a spare tablet she mostly used for watching Netflix or Amazon Prime when she was on a train or bus, or stuck in traffic.

As she stood by the door, looking back at the bare bones of her flat, she wondered if she would ever be back.

The council worker was still waiting outside.

'Sorry,' she said. 'I … ah, had a lot of things.'

'No problem, Miss. If you give that number on your phone a call back in the morning, you can get more details. Do you need a lift up to the City Lodge?'

The hotel was close enough that its upper floors were visible over the top of the trees at the end of the street.

'No, I'll walk,' she said, then didn't walk, just stood and stared as the council worker picked up his bag. He headed for his van, but just before he got there, he stopped, glanced at Old Len, who was sitting on the bench by the edge of the park, muttering to himself, then wandered over.

'Hey mate, you hungry?' Lily heard him say. 'You want to go and get sausage and chips?'

She couldn't hear Old Len's reply, or even if there was one, but the council worker nodded. 'No probs. I'll bring you back a takeaway. You want peas or beans?'

Again, the old tramp's reply was lost, but the council worker nodded, then went back to his van. Lily watched it pull away, glanced at Old Len, still muttering to himself on the bench, then slowly began to walk up the street.

5

DEFLATED

THE CITY LODGE WAS COMFORTABLE—IF BLAND—AND her room actually had a better view than the one from her solitary flat window. The breakfast—included, thankfully; dropping nearly twenty quid every morning would have certainly got to work on her savings pretty fast—was as good as the council worker had said, although Lily found she had little appetite. Sitting in the lobby afterwards, however, she watched the business travellers marching back and forth, and decided she needed to be positive.

Headhunted by Davidon's through a university careers programme, she had never actually had to apply for a job, but although it was a depressingly bland process, by the time she was four coffees deep out of the hotel's daytime cafeteria, she had put applications in at more than a dozen financial institutions. Something was missing though, and it was only as she applied for yet another financial advisory management position that she began to wonder what had happened to the colour in her life.

She got up, intending to refill her coffee cup for a fifth time, and caught a glimpse of herself in one of the reflective pillars that presumably prevented the hotel from crashing down on her head.

Grey from head to toe. Even her hair—light brown—seemed to reflect the grey business suit she had worn out of habit. She looked pretty enough, she supposed, but could have walked onto the set of a black and white movie without any complaint.

Being positive was something her parents had always instilled in her, so she put away her laptop and stood up. What could she do to cheer herself up? Mentally, she started to make a list:

Buy something with flowers on it

Buy some actual flowers

Buy a box of doughnuts

Do all of the above

Go wedding dress shopping

Perfect. She clicked her fingers. Steve would be at his studio on Lower Castle Road, and there was a Mister Donut nearby. Doughnuts, a surprise visit, and then an afternoon of wedding shopping together. Then, hopefully to top it all off, she would open her laptop in the evening to find her email simply pinging with job interview requests.

She would need to squeeze in a visit to the zoo to make it a perfect day, but she'd wasted too much time drinking coffee, so would have to settle for a nearly. Perhaps they could feed some stray cats or something.

Steve's studio was in an attic apartment overlooking a canal. At least three times the size of her own place, it had decent views, high rafters, and even a balcony. When she had suggested they might convert it into a first home after their wedding, however, Steve had stared wide-eyed and said, 'Marriage is supposed to be a beginning, not an end,' whatever that might mean, so Lily had dropped it. He was close, though, close to breaking through, so he said, to getting a big exhibition or a major commission. One day, he said, she'd look back on the years supporting him and see them as worth it. And, of course, you had to support your partner. That's what real couples did.

She picked up five doughnuts—two each and one for luck—then found herself whistling as she went into his building's lobby. There was a small dress shop up the street where she thought they could start, and she glanced through the catalogue she had picked up while she waited for the lift—another luxury she couldn't afford for herself.

As the lift doors opened, she smelled the aroma of oil paints and clay. The landlord had complained to her on several occasions, but Lily had liked it. Not only did it feel familiar, but it reminded her of home. Her mother was always making something, and when he wasn't running a burger van, her dad's hobby was creating murals out of stones or glass. Lily, who had never really been into anything creative, might have worried she was adopted, had it not been that she had both her mother's looks and her father's determination, not to mention a bit of both noses.

Steve's door was locked, and Lily didn't have a key, despite paying Steve's monthly rent. He said a creative should never be interrupted, and who was she to argue? A person on a business call didn't like to be interrupted either.

However, today she felt like surprising him. She pressed the buzzer, then put a finger over the little camera.

'Who is it?' came Steve's voice.

Lily frowned, then attempted to put on a man's voice. 'It's the council,' she said, trying not to laugh.

'Oh, right. Well, hang on a minute.'

Steve opened the door and stepped back. Before he could react, Lily jumped forward, into his arms.

'Lily … what's this all about? It's really not a good time … I was in the middle of something.'

His body felt rigid. He had put one hand on her back, but there was none of the warmth she would usually feel. She let go of him, noticing that the belt of his jeans was unbuckled beneath his untucked shirt.

Unruly and unkempt where she could have stepped out of a business attire catalogue, it wasn't unusual. As she pulled away, however, Lily caught movement out of the corner of her eye.

'Well, Steven,' came a curt woman's voice. 'I'll be in touch.'

Lily felt the air move as Steve tensed. She turned. A woman several years older than herself with a stern but flushed face and the buttons of her blouse undone was making for the door.

'Who are you?'

'This is … ah … Margaret from Billings Street Gallery,' Steve said. 'We're … ah … negotiating for an exhibition.'

The stairs to the lower floors—against fire regulations which would get her another slap on the wrist if the landlord found out—were blocked, so there was another awkward moment while Margaret pressed the lift door control, then had to wait a few seconds for the doors to open. She glanced back at Steve as she went inside, then the doors closed, and Lily felt her world collapsing.

'I can explain—'

The doughnuts tumbled from her hand as Lily turned. One hand came up, and she slapped him across the cheek with all the power she could muster, which admittedly, slightly off balance, wasn't much. He staggered, letting out a theatrical gasp.

'It's not what it looks like,' he cried. 'Sometimes, you

have do what needs to be done. Don't tell me no one's ever slept their way to the top in the finance industry—'

She stepped back and slammed the door. She wanted to kill him, but nothing blocking the stairs looked like a suitable weapon. She jabbed the lift door control, but the old thing was still in the process of taking Margaret from Billings Street Gallery out of her life, so instead Lily clambered up the pile of folded easels and paint points and sheets and other junk that she had spent the last three years paying for, until she could get to the stairs beyond. Then, trying not to cry, she ran down them as fast as she could, doing her best not to slip in her heels and add a visit to the emergency room to the growing list of bad luck that was stacking up on her shoulders like a precarious pile of folded chairs.

An expensive car was just pulling away from the curb. Lily looked around for something to throw, but this section of road was uncommonly neat and tidy, and all she could do was lift a frustrated fist and hope Margaret from Billings Street Gallery—if indeed it was actually a place—would glance in the mirror just before she turned out of sight. Somehow, Lily doubted it.

She had to get away. Steve would no doubt come after her, wrap his arms around her, unveil a few creative excuses and get himself back in her good books. The most worrying thing, however, was that she knew she would fall for it. When nothing about her life any longer seemed stable, she would grasp for whatever stability she could find, and he would be back in her life, forgiven.

Not this time.

She staggered down a path to a towpath alongside the canal, a pretty, flower-lined place with wrought iron benches and ducks waiting to be fed where they had spent many a summer evening muttering sweet nothings and musing on their long and eventful future together. Where they would live, what they would do, how many children they would have. Lily felt like the world was spinning faster and faster, ready to throw her off. She grabbed on to a stone wall surrounding a flowerbed and waiting for a wave of dizziness to pass.

Something buzzed in the purse still slung over her shoulder.

Her phone.

She pulled it out. A picture of her and Steve together in front of the Tate Gallery was pulsing on the screen.

It had started already. He was probably in the lift now, perhaps as far as the lobby, looking for her, wondering where she had gone.

Her feet felt made of stone. She pushed away from the flowerbed but couldn't move, as though she were trapped. Soon he would find her, and the excuses would start.

Screaming, she pulled back her hand and tossed her mobile into the canal. Almost at once the hold over her felt broken, and she found herself running up the towpath, up a set of steps onto a bridge over the canal, down another road, away from everything.

When exhaustion made her pull up, she felt something she hadn't felt in forever.

Free.

What to do now? She had no home or job, and her boyfriend was a cheating, sponging pig. She had no hope except to press reset and try to build it all up again: find another tiny flat, another soulless job, another worthless boyfriend.

Lily shook her head. There had to be more to life than this. But what? She had just thrown her access to the world into the murky waters of an East London canal.

She walked on a little further, no longer sure what she

was doing or where she was going. There, at the end of the street, was a phone box.

Not really sure what she was doing, she went inside, felt a momentary relief that the phone was still in working order, then dropped a pound into the coin slot and called the only number she could remember by heart.

The dial tone pulsed in her ear. Lily wasn't sure what she would do if no one answered.

Then: 'Hello?'

Lily wanted to cry. 'Dad? It's me, Lily. I'm not doing too well. I think I need a little help....'

6

———

HOMECOMING

WITH ALL HER WORLDLY POSSESSIONS IN A SUITCASE AT her feet, her hopes and dreams floating somewhere in a drain nearby, Lily was waiting outside the City Lodge when her parents' car pulled up. Pete Markham wound down the driver's window and leaned out.

'Taxi for a wonderful but struggling young lady?'

'Dad!'

He climbed out and they shared a warm embrace, before he opened the passenger door for her and then put her case into the back.

'Your mother's cooking dinner,' he said, as he started the car and turned out of the hotel's car park. 'We're both so glad you're coming home.'

'You didn't have to pick me up,' Lily said. 'I could have got the train.'

'Not when my little girl's upset,' Pete said. 'Although, I was thinking of picking you up in the van, just for a laugh.'

'How is the mobile catering industry?'

'Lively,' Pete said. 'Sycamore Park has been busy this year, and I've had a lot of private bookings.'

'And the side project?'

'Well, I've had a couple of commissions,' Pete said. 'It's not big money, but it's only a hobby, isn't it?'

'That's good. A couple more than Steve has ever had.'

'I gather things haven't gone to plan?'

'No.'

'Would you like to do a detour so I can throw him in the river?'

Lily shook her head. 'No, it's all right. I nailed him pretty hard. And this morning I cancelled the tenancy on his studio. He has a month to find somewhere else … and of course the money to pay for it.'

'Your mother and I were never happy about you supporting him,' Pete said. 'I know you were in love and all that, but we both thought he was a bit of a scrounger.'

Had her dad said such a thing a week ago, Lily would have vehemently defended Steve, but now she felt like a deflated balloon. 'I suppose we all make mistakes, don't we?'

'Too true. Now you sit back and relax, so that I don't make another trying to get out of this godforsaken city. Whoever plans these places needs a kick up the backside.'

They stopped at Fleet Services because her dad wanted a pasty, then stopped again an hour later because Pete wanted a quick walk around Stonehenge, 'Since it's kind of on the way, isn't it?'

It was a warm afternoon, the air fresh and less muggy than was usual in London, and Lily enjoyed the walk around the giant stone circle, before they got a coffee and a rock cake in the café inside the visitor centre.

'Do you want to talk about it?' Pete said as they idled

away the afternoon, looking out of the recently built café at the flat Wiltshire landscape, the massive stone rectangles nowhere in sight. 'I mean, you might want to make a mental list of what you could talk to me about and what you should leave for your mother, but if you want to….'

Lily sighed. 'I feel like I drove my car off a cliff.'

Pete smiled. 'I imagine you'd need to pour some water over yourself or something to claim that. You had a bad run, that's all.'

'Bad? I lost my job, my house, and my fiancé in the space of a couple of days.'

Pete nodded. 'Yep, that's the three. So you should be safe now.'

'What?'

'Bad things always happen in threes. You've got all yours out of the way, so you're good to go. I reckon you could walk across the M3 blindfolded in fog and make it to the other side.'

Lily forced a smile. 'Thanks, Dad. I know you're trying to make me feel better.'

Pete leaned forward. 'Or, you could look at it not as three bad things, but three good things.'

'What do you mean?'

'Look, I know you got paid well, but your job was about as soulless as they come. Your flat—sure, it was pretty central for London—was a glorified shoebox, and Steve—well, I kind of liked him, with the art thing going on and all that—but he was a total sponge. I mean, I tolerated him, but your mother thought he was a clown of the highest order, and this from a woman who spends her days making dreamcatchers out of twigs and feathers.'

'And selling them for ten quid a pop. Perhaps she'll give me a job in her workshop?'

'If you ask nicely. I'm not sure she could afford your salary bracket, though.'

'Everything feels unreal, like the last four years was a weird dream and I just woke up. I don't know what to do.'

'You'll find another job, and another boyfriend, and your flat will be fixed up in no time.'

'Don't forget the car. Oh, that makes four.'

'Ah, but both your car and your flat can be fixed, so they only count as a half each.'

'Dad … you're totally shoehorning now.'

Pete smiled. 'You've just had a bad run. We all get them. Remember that time I hit my thumb with a hammer in the morning, then broke my toe in the afternoon when the car rolled off the jack?'

'What was number three?'

Pete frowned. 'Your mother cooked that god-awful spinach pie for dinner.'

'I thought you liked that?'

'I liked it more than I like upsetting your mother.' Pete shrugged. 'It's passable if you douse it with enough salad cream. Talking of food, this cheesecake is pretty top notch. Shall we go halves on another?'

'Sure, why not?'

An hour later, after another quick walk around Stonehenge, they headed further southwest and down into Devon. Only as she started to see the old signs of home, a copse of familiar trees here, a distant manor house there, the sign for Exeter, and then the much smaller one to Brentwell and Willow River, did Lily realise how much she had missed it. Caught on the relentless treadmill of London life, she hadn't been home in over two years, even skipping out a traditional family Christmas to let Steve take her off to Lapland for the holiday, one where her dreams of seeing the aurora had been dashed by relentless snow and finally by a power failure which had seen them evacuated from their glass ceilinged igloo hotel into a bland concrete monstrosity near the airport. And now, as they crossed the little bridge with its slightly wonky sign announcing

WILLOW RIVER
Twinned with Rivers Everywhere

Lily felt a weight lift off her heart. The memories came rushing back to greet her like old friends. The day Tim Johnson from the Sixth Year had sprayed "Except the Thames, because it's polluted" on the sign and been given a police caution; the time when, a month after passing her driving test, she had driven her dad's car too fast at the little humpback bridge and broken off the front bumper; the canoeing trip in the Fifth Year when the plan had been to canoe along Willow River right into Exeter, only for the teachers to pick drought season, meaning after carrying the canoes for half a mile along a river too shallow for them to float, they had given up, called up the bus, and gone to a museum instead.

'What are you smiling about?' Pete asked.

'Nothing,' Lily said. 'Just glad to be home.'

They passed the church where she'd spent a summer painstakingly making sketches for a school project; the village green where she'd once won a trophy at the yearly carnival for winning the Under-14s skittles tournament; the leafy garden behind the Bennett's place where she'd shared her first kiss with Simon Bennett, a boy two years older, and—the last she'd heard, at any rate—now serving in the RAF. Beyond that was a cul-de-sac down which her schooldays best friend Mary Wilson had lived, and possibly still did.

'Got two kids now,' Pete said, as though reading her mind, then sighed. 'Didn't call either of them Peter. Sliding down the league tables, now.'

'If I ever have a boy, I'll at least put it on my list,' Lily said.

'You're a love.'

The road angled through the tiny village centre, past a pub where Lily had got drunk for the first time, and the beer garden at the back where she had first thrown up; down a gentle hill towards the Willow River valley and passed the turning to Uncle Gus's guesthouse. They crossed the river again over a little bridge where Lily and her friends had once picked up great handfuls of frogspawn in the shallows, then up another gentle hill through meandering lanes. They passed a small car park with half a dozen cars parked against the hedge, then Pete turned them left down a narrow lane.

'There's the old girl,' he said, pulling up outside a gate.

'Still looking good, Dad,' Lily said, smiling at the sight of Pete's burger van, parked in a lay-by just outside their drive.

And then she was home, back to the quaint cottage that she had grown up in, with its three-hundred-and-sixty degree garden, its cob walls and thatched roof that was one of the last of its kind in the area. While Willow River, with its quaint shops and cycle path that led all the way to Exeter via Brentwell, grew more popular with tourists every year, Lily had seen more than the odd tourist taking photos from the end of their drive.

'Is Mum at the shop?'

Pete glanced at his watch. 'No, she should be back by now.'

Almost as if on cue, the front door opened and Sarah Markham appeared. Lily's mother had dyed her hair again, with the original brown long gone, replaced by a slightly reddish auburn with a couple of strands of purple thrown in for good measure. Lily climbed out of the car and ran up the path, into her mother's embrace.

'So, my little girl needs a bit of a getaway,' Sarah said. 'Darling, it's lovely to have you home.'

'Thanks, Mum.'

'I've put the My Little Pony bedspread back on your bed to make you feel comfortable.'

'Seriously?'

Sarah barked a laugh. 'No, it went to the jumble sale years ago. But don't worry, maybe I can paint you something on the wall if necessary.'

'I think I'll be all right.'

Sarah let go of Lily and opened the door. 'Well, let's get you inside. You've had a long journey and you must be starving. I didn't have time to go to the supermarket, but I've managed to rustle something up.'

'Oh, what?'

'I baked one of those spinach pies that your father really likes.'

OLD FRIEND

AT FIRST, AS AUGUST'S LINGERING HEAT BEGAN TO FADE away into September's cool mornings and sudden thunderstorms, Lily couldn't bring herself to go outside. She lay on her bed or sat in the living room watching TV, trying not to think about anything too deeply. Since throwing her phone into the river outside Steve's place, she had maintained radio silence, refusing to go online or even get around to sorting out a replacement phone. Every morning she had woken to the sound of her mother doing a body combat exercise DVD in the living room, then ambled downstairs to eat breakfast with her father before he went off in his burger van to work. Then, for the rest of the day she had either watched TV or pottered about in the garden, weeding flowerbeds, tidying up the vegetable plot, cutting back some of the hedges which had got a little overgrown.

As a few days turned into a week, then into two, Lily knew that sooner or later she was going to have to venture back out into the world.

The day she finally decided to do it was a rainy

Monday halfway through September. She got dressed and came downstairs to find her Mum in gym shorts and a Reebok t-shirt being shouted at by a woman in combat fatigues on the TV.

'Come on, worms, work harder!' the woman hollered. 'I can see you out there slacking off, stopping to sip your milk like a bunch of pansies. You know how you survive in the prison yard? Lift those knees higher!'

'Would you like to join me?' Sarah gasped, as Lily picked up a DVD case from the arm of the sofa and read, *Doreen's Prison Yard Boot Camp Volume 3.*

'I'll be all right, but don't give up, Mum. Doreen's watching you.'

'Coffee in the pot,' Sarah gasped in response.

Her dad had already gone out to work, so Lily sat at the table with a coffee and a bowl of cornflakes, and read a copy of yesterday's Daily Mail. Then, stealing herself, she headed for the front door.

It was drizzling a little, but nothing an umbrella, wellington boots, and a light raincoat couldn't handle.

The nostalgia was almost too much as Lily made her way back up the road, pausing by the old phone box on the corner—now turned into a local art display and featuring a couple of her mother's dreamcatchers and a little mural her dad had made out of broken pieces of glass glued onto plywood—remembering the years she had stood here for the school bus to take her into Brentwell, and the years before that when she had waited for Jimmy Donbury, the farmer's son who lived further up the hill, and Christina Sinkins, who had lived down a street opposite. Every day for nearly five years the three of them had walked to school together, until eventually Christina's family had moved up to Liverpool, and Jimmy, who was two years older, had gone to the local comprehensive, leaving Lily, by then nine, to walk to Willow River Primary—tucked in behind the church—for the last two years alone.

She walked on down the hill, the hedgerows and trees exactly as she remembered—although the Donburys had finally replaced a gate that had been collapsed and overgrown—even some of the same potholes in the road, where she had poked sticks and sometimes, in moments of kindness, filled with rocks from along the verge.

Wondering how much more she could handle, it was something of a relief to reach the car park and its lane that accessed the cycle path. She didn't remember the branch line from when trains had still run—the line having closed in 2003, when she was just seven years old—but for most of her childhood it had been an impassible mass of brambles. A council initiative had turned it into a cycle path back in her mid-teens, at the same time turning Willow River into something of a tourist attraction. Uncle Gus's guesthouse, which had once overlooked a railway line and a particularly dull section of river, suddenly found itself surrounded by picnic areas and viewing spots. In close proximity to the Willow River entrance and exit, Uncle Gus had needed to expand his restaurant and open up several rooms that had previously been filled with junk. What had once been a quiet B&B in the middle of nowhere was now something of a resort hotel for middle-aged couples extending themselves with a bit of countryside bike riding.

She crossed the little bridge at the bottom, where a new stop sign now stood and speed bumps to halt any boy racers looking to mow down a few cyclists, and headed up the hill into the little village. Her mother's craft shop on the corner next to a café was closed, a sign over the door giving working hours of 10 a.m. to 4 p.m. The rain had got progressively heavier, and despite the taste of coffee still lingering on her tongue, Lily couldn't resist going into the café, which had just opened, for a quick pit stop.

It was empty, but as she folded her umbrella and took off her jacket, a gasp came from behind her.

'Huh. Well, I'll never. Hello, stranger.'

Lily looked up. Behind the counter stood an older—and pregnant version—of a familiar face.

'Mary? Mary Wilson? Is that you?'

'It's Mary Stone now.' Mary smiled as she came out from behind the counter and waddled over to where Lily stood, shell-shocked, by the door. 'But you were close enough.'

They shared a warm hug, and Lily felt the years shift again, taking her back to nights in the pub, and beyond that to school days, whispering about boys in the playground, proclaiming with complete certainty that Mrs. Davies had a dragon in the closet in their First Year classroom, tears as both slipped in the mud on a primary school forest walk, and cheers as their three-legged bundle came home first in the final race of their first school sports day.

Mary stepped back. She had aged, two kids and a third on the way having added years to her, but that old easygoing manner was still there. Her hair, tied back in a neat if unadorned ponytail, looked a little thinner, even with a premature strand or two of grey, but her eyes were bright with life and excitement.

'You look well,' Mary said. 'Well, your eyes are a bit puffy and you've got a scratch on your chin. Oh, and tints in your hair. But you look like you live off cucumbers and carrots. Are you back for a visit or for longer?'

'To be honest, I don't know.'

'Well, it's chucking down, and it's not likely to stop for a few hours. We'll get old Mrs. Gregson in for her coffee about lunchtime, but most of the grockles will stay away. How about I get you a large coffee and you can catch me up while I struggle to stay awake on a pansy decaf?'

'Sounds good.'

Mary waved Lily to a table near the counter, and the years rolled off both as they talked easily about the past. Friends since being forced to hold hands in the dinner queue in reception class, their lives had followed an easily meandering side-by-side course until they'd reached sixth form, where they had dramatically diverged. Lily had stayed and then gone on to university, never to return, while Mary had taken a horticulture course in Exeter college and then married one of her fellow students, who now managed a garden centre just outside of Brentwell. Her first boy, Sylvian, had been born when she was twenty, her second, Ryan, two years later. After a four year gap, she was hoping the next would be a little girl.

'Ryan literally started school last week,' Mary said, affectionately rubbing her stomach. 'The first day, he really didn't want to go. They had to practically drag him out of my arms. The second day, though, I couldn't hold him back. He loves it now. He's supposed to finish at lunchtime for the first term, but we signed him up for the after-school programme, so I go and pick the boys up at the same time, after Jan arrives to cover the afternoon.' She leaned forward, cupping her chin on her hands. 'So, what about you? Don't tell me you haven't got tons of guys after you. I did notice the depression on your ring finger. Did you forget to put it on?'

Lily closed her eyes for a moment. The hurt had eased over the last couple of weeks, but mentioning it directly was like pouring salt into an open wound.

'Things didn't work out,' she said. 'He turned out to be a scumbag.'

'Ah, you'll find someone else. You're still young.'

'I'm not looking.'

Mary gave another easy smile. 'Neither was I. Was planning to open a little business or something, but it all fell into my lap, and I wouldn't change it for the world.'

Her old friend's blissful happiness made Lily feel a little strange. Not only was there the nostalgia to deal with, but also the feeling that the divergence in their lives had been permanent. They had chosen different paths, and while they might still fondly wave at each other from a distance, or occasionally meet up to reminisce, there was no going back. They would never be the friends they had been. Part of Lily wished she had never left, while another part wished she had never come back.

She declined the offer of another coffee, claiming some undefined list of chores her mother had given her. They embraced by the door, both promising to meet up sometime soon, a meeting Lily expected would never happen. As she went out, hearing the little ping of the door bell as the door closed behind her, she felt like she had closed another chapter of her life, without opening up any doors to another. She felt a strange urge to cry.

'What am I doing?' she wondered aloud. 'Why did I leave, and why did I come back?'

WORK EXPERIENCE

'WHY DON'T YOU COME FOR A JOG?' SARAH SAID, stretching her arms out to the side as though to catch Lily's attention. 'Get rid of all that negative energy. You've been pulsing with it all afternoon.'

Lily propped her chin up on her hand and tried to sit up straight. 'I walked around the village today. That's a start, isn't it?'

'And now it's time to *run* around the village.'

Lily grimaced. 'Maybe tomorrow.'

'Come on....'

The front door opened and a cheerful whistle announced Pete's return from work. Lily smiled as her dad came in, shrugged his coat off his shoulders, gave Sarah a peck on the cheek, then slipped into a chair with the grace of a stage actor, propping one foot over the other and then lifting an eyebrow.

'How was your day, dear?'

Lily scowled. 'Frustrating. I felt like I was bouncing back and forth between wishing I'd never left and wishing I'd never come back. All the people from school still around have moved on. We don't have anything in common anymore. And all the new stuff … it makes me feel like I've missed out. I don't know whether I'm coming or going.'

'Ah, that's to be expected,' Pete said. 'You know what I think?'

'She needs more exercise,' Sarah said.

'That's one possibility. However, it's not just that.'

'What, Dad?'

Pete smiled. 'You tell me, sweetheart.'

Lily frowned. 'I need … I need to … I need to find some kind of … purpose.'

Pete clicked his fingers together. 'Tomorrow is Saturday. I take the van to Sycamore Park in Brentwell on a Saturday, and it looks like the weather is going to brighten up.' He put on his most needy face. 'I could really do with some help….'

'You want me to flip burgers?'

'And brew cheap coffee, open packets of disposable cups, scoop chips out of the portable freezer.' Pete spread his arms. 'A whole manner of things.'

'I haven't done anything like that since I worked for a summer behind the bar in The Crown,' Lily said.

'So, now's your chance. Time to see how us paupers live.'

'You're not a pauper, Dad.'

'I'll accept yeoman farmer. After all, the potatoes went great this year.'

'We did have a few decent weeks of sun,' Sarah agreed. 'Right, I'll see you later. This butt won't tighten itself.'

'Good luck,' Pete said, grinning as Lily cringed.

'So, you really want me to help you?'

'I'll pay you. I don't expect you to work for free.'

Lily smiled. 'How much?'

'Friends and family rate. Fiver an hour.'

Running a portable burger van was a lot harder than Lily had expected. The day started long before they actually had to sell anything, with checking the van itself for fuel and supplies, making sure they had enough power for the generator, checking the sell-by dates on the food, making sure everything was clean and well-organised.

'Last thing you want is some council idiot having a go over a grease stain,' Pete said, as they climbed up into the cab and headed out.

Lily remembered Sycamore Park from her secondary school days. Having caught a school bus from Willow River, she hadn't spent much time there except when visiting friends who lived locally, but, particularly in the early years there had been regular picnics, as well as various events and festivals through the year. At Christmas there was always a small market for a couple of weeks, and on summer evenings lights were sometimes hung from the trees. In autumn though, it really looked its best, when all the leaves started to turn, and every gust of wind brought showers of red and gold leaves.

Pete's van stood by the south entrance, and within minutes of setting up, a small queue had begun to form.

'Poor buggers them who've got to work on a Saturday,' Pete said, giving Lily a wink while greeting another middle-aged man with a business suit hidden under a jacket, who was rubbing his hands to ward off the morning chill. 'Coffee and a sausage bap, is it, mate?'

Most people seemed to know Pete, and Lily couldn't help but feel a pang of longing at the way her father warmly greeted people from all walks of life, from a man in a Gucci suit whose haircut had probably cost as much as the van, to a girl in her late teens whose jeans had frays that weren't designer, and whose dirty trainers had laces of different colours. Lily watched proudly as Pete slipped an extra sausage into the girl's roll and overpaid her change.

Try as she might, though, Lily was struggling to handle the simplicity of cooking a burger that wasn't black on the outside, or pink on the inside, or remembering which Tupperware pot was sugar and which was salt.

'Dad, you should replace the labels,' she said in frustration, as, halfway up the path leading to a duck pond, a customer they had just served took a sip of his coffee and then spat it out, before throwing a sour look over his shoulder and dumping the rest of the cup's contents into the nearest hedge. 'All I can see is two faded S's.'

'That bit's a corner of an A,' Pete said, pointing to a smear on a faded label. 'Don't worry, he wasn't a regular. If you're not sure, just dip your finger in.'

'Isn't that against health and safety?'

'Only if they're watching.' Pete grinned. 'A few germs never hurt anyone. Ask literally any kid who grew up between the fifties and the nineties.'

'I burned that last burger too,' Lily said.

'That's why I put extra ketchup in. Don't worry, he didn't notice. Most people are in too much of a hurry to care.'

'I'm useless at this.'

'You'll get better. Just give it time.'

Lily enjoyed chatting to some of the customers, but she wasn't sad when Pete decided to close just after the lunchtime rush was over. When Lily asked if their own lunch would be burgers and sausage baps, Pete shook his head.

'Not a chance. We'll go and get some proper food.'

Beside the park's northern entrance stood a delightful restaurant called the Oak Leaf Café, where its charming owner, an older lady called Angela, greeted Pete like an old friend. Lily had expected some kind of rivalry, but they chatted about the day's customers and then Angela served them a delicious pie with roasted seasonal vegetables.

'You should sell stuff like this,' Lily told Pete as they ate.

'Ah, different catchment group,' Pete said. 'Plus, I don't want to step on Angela's toes.'

Before they left, Angela brought over a cardboard box.

'I found these in a charity shop,' she said. 'I immediately thought of you.'

Pete opened the top of the box and smiled. 'Fantastic. Thanks a lot.'

The box was full of multi-coloured pieces of glass and plastic, as though someone had smashed a set of traffic lights and collected the pieces. Lily had often wondered where her dad got the pieces for the mosaics he liked to make in the old shed behind their house, but Pete was beaming as they headed back across the park to the van.

'These'll keep me going for ages,' he said.

'Do people often just give you stuff they find?' Lily asked.

'If they know you're looking,' he said. 'Life's all about connections, isn't it? The more you have, the better.'

On the way home, they both agreed that Lily hadn't exactly impressed during her first stint working on the family burger van. She promised to try harder the following day, but Pete shook his head.

'I think we need to add a bit of variation to your life,'

he said. 'You can take tomorrow off, and then on Monday you can help your mother in the shop.'

'Dad ... you know we'd end up needling each other,' Lily said. 'You know what we're like together.'

Pete shrugged. 'It's been a few years.'

'Too few, I imagine.'

Lily had spent a summer working with Sarah in the little craft shop, but her mother's propensity to "artify" her sales technique had driven Lily nearly out of her mind. Prices were rarely advertised, and when they were Sarah would discount at random depending on how close a friend she considered the customer. Somehow, the shop still made a profit, but the unorthodox method of business had driven Lily—fresh from A stars at mathematics, physics and business studies—near out of her mind.

Pete clicked his fingers. 'I have an idea,' he said. 'Let me make a phone call when we get home.'

It was raining again as they reached Willow River, the large, hanging trees in the park in the valley below their house swaying in a growing wind. Lily sighed as she looked out of the window. There was something intensely nostalgic about autumn storms. When the tourists left and the town became the sole property of the local people again, when the days grew shorter and the leaves started to change ... that was what made her feel at home. The summer was always just a fleeting moment. The off-season, with its long days of rain, chilly mornings, occasional crispy clear skies and dawn sunlight glinting off a garden glittering with frost ... that was what felt real.

Pete went straight inside, leaving Lily to tidy up the van. By the time she had followed him in, he was sitting by the table, a coffee in front of him, wearing a wide smile.

'I just got off the phone with Uncle Gus,' he said. 'You start tomorrow.'

9

WILLOW RIVER GUESTHOUSE

UNCLE GUS WAS LILY'S DAD'S OLDER BROTHER. MUCH older, in fact. Lily wasn't exactly sure, but there was at least fifteen years between them, Pete's arrival being something of a thrilling surprise, she remembered her late grandmother telling her. In fact, Grandma had been willing to share far too many details for Lily's liking, even if in retrospect it made her miss the old dear even more.

'We'd gone down to the Village Hall for a barn dance, then on the way back your grandfather started getting a little frisky.'

'Please, stop—'

Grandma chuckled. 'He wanted to nip into the park down there and have a private dance by the riverside. It wasn't until we got there that I realised what kind of dance he meant….'

'Grandma, I have to go and do my maths homework, or alternatively find some knitting needles to shove into my ears.'

Grandma, by then in her mid-eighties, had patted Lily's knee and nearly fallen off her chair.

'And nine months later your father appeared,' she said, waving her arthritic hands about as though he'd literally appeared out of the air. 'And from day one he was a little treasure. He had his off days, though. Did I ever tell you about that time he managed to undo his own nappy on the slide at playschool? He turned that orange slide brown—'

Lily smiled at the memory. It was one of the last conversations she could remember with Grandma, who had died when she was twelve. Uncle Gus had got the guesthouse, Pete her grandparents' cottage, plus a cut of the guesthouse's profits, she had found out years later. It was one of the reasons her parents managed to maintain such a beautiful property on two seemingly low-income jobs.

On the other hand, however, it meant they had to keep one eye on the eccentric Uncle Gus and how well the guesthouse was doing.

Built into a tree-lined hollow at the top of a gentle hill leading down to the river, Willow River Guesthouse had long been the centerpiece of the village. Pete had told her how growing up it had doubled as the local community centre before a separate one was built and had hosted everything from local weddings and funerals to parish council elections. When the great storm of 1987 had put out all the local power lines, Grandpa had fired up a couple of auxiliary generators and invited the whole village to stay. Even Lily, not yet born, had heard tales of the party that resulted, and Pete had once jokingly told her that 1988 had seen a local baby boom and a slew of shotgun marriages.

For most of its existence, however, it had been a quaint family-run hotel, just nine rooms which were rarely fully booked, and a pretty restaurant with views over the river and the railway line alongside. The railway's closure had hit the business hard, but just as dips follow booms, booms can follow dips, and the opening of the cycle route to Exeter had restored the guesthouse to its former glory, as well as boosting its year-round trade.

Lily, dressed in jeans and a light sweater under her jacket, politely refused Pete's offer of a lift, preferring to walk the half a mile down through the valley and up to the guesthouse's long, paved driveway that meandered up the hill between two lines of willows which had already begun to shed some of their autumn leaves. The car park to the side was almost full, a couple of the cars blanketed in fallen leaves as though their owners had arrived and never left.

A glass conservatory pushed out from the rest of the old grey-brick building, surrounded by so many thorny roses that Sleeping Beauty's castle might have been jealous. A narrow path led between them on one side up to a front door.

Lily opened the door and stepped inside, a little bell jingling to announce her arrival. She was greeted by the smell of nostalgia: musty carpets and dusty antiques, every wall and available surface adorned by an array of ancient artifacts that Grandpa had once made a hobby of collecting. Every room in the guesthouse was a collector's heaven, with ancient toy cars set alongside collections of 1950s toasters, or wrought iron gilt mirrors reflecting dusty faces, train posters from the 1920s alongside war memorabilia and framed letters so faded their copperplate words were illegible. A mounted deer's head protruded from among a cluster of rusty antique kettles hung from the ceiling, and a cupboard facing the entrance held plates and cups that hadn't been used for their original purpose in a hundred years or more.

'Uncle Gus? Aunt Gert?'

No answer. Lily took off her shoes as was required of

all guests, and put them into a cupboard for shoes beside the door. There were several other pairs there, some that looked expensive. Then, stepping up onto an old threadbare carpet, she made her way into the guesthouse.

A downstairs living area had a square of sofas around a coffee table laden with books and magazines on antique furniture. An old gramophone sat on a scored mahogany table in one corner, near a tall lacquered chest of drawers. More shelves of ornaments filled every available space; lines of Russian matryoshka dolls, metal American classic car toys, stuffed bears and dolls, their clothes and fur faded, stared blankly into space, as though remembering joyful children now long dead.

'Is anyone here?'

Finally, Lily heard movement from behind a door leading to the guesthouse kitchens. The door creaked open and the soft thud of footfalls approached. Lily's heart raced before her uncle's basset hound, Rufus, padded into view from behind a chest of drawers, looked up at her with delightfully sad eyes, gave a quick sniff and then let his tongue loll in greeting.

'Hello there, old guy,' Lily said, leaning down to pet the dog she hadn't seen since leaving for university eight years before. In those days, Rufus would have gladly waddled after a tennis ball tossed across the field outside. Now, after allowing her a couple of minutes of fuss, he headed back to a basket just behind the door.

Lily pushed open the door into the kitchens and peered inside. 'Hello? It's Lily. Anyone about?'

'Boo!' came a sudden cry from behind her, followed by a howl of laughter as Lily, terrified, crashed forward into a line of hanging pans, managing to catch one as it slipped off its hook and came tumbling down. She turned, heart racing, only to find Uncle Gus, dressed in a sky-blue apron and wearing an equally sky-blue chef's hat, bellowing with laughter.

'Ah, Lillian, dear, had you going there. Probably thought this place was haunted, didn't you? Nope, still full of life after all these years.' Uncle Gus's thick beard, protected by an upside-down hair net, shook as he turned to the kitchen. 'Gert, she's here. You can tell the guests to come back inside now.'

Lily was still too shocked to speak. She looked down at Rufus in his basket, the old dog lifting an ear as though to acknowledge her as a co-sufferer, before settling back down and closing his eyes.

'We've all been expecting you,' Uncle Gus said, waving Lily to follow him into the kitchen. He had put on even more weight since Lily had last seen him, his body brushing the walls as he walked, his towering frame causing hanging pots to clang and clatter. As he led her into a kitchen incongruously bright compared to the rest of the guesthouse, Aunt Gert appeared through a glass door leading into the conservatory, waving a handful of rather disgruntled-looking guests back into the indoor restaurant area.

'Everyone, this is my little niece,' Aunt Gert said to the handful of middle-aged and elderly guests, none of which seemed particularly interested. 'Hasn't she grown?'

Lily hadn't actually grown at all since she had last seen her aunt. Gertrude, however, was as small as Uncle Gus was big, a tiny grey-haired thing who barely reached Lily's shoulders. Like some kind of human hamster, all Lily could ever remember her eating at family parties through her teenage years were carrot and cucumber sticks, and she looked light enough that Lily could have carried one of her over each shoulder. As her hands reached up and patted

Lily's cheeks, however, Lily felt a wiry strength borne from long hours of hotel work.

'Right,' Uncle Gus said, clapping his hands together with a meaty thud. 'Let's get these breakfasts done. Lily, you're on eggs. Ever fried one?'

'Ah … a couple of times.'

'Gert, how many do we need?'

'Thirteen.'

Uncle Gus pointed at a wide stainless steel area that Lily had taken to be a work surface. 'Switch is on the wall. Let's make these campers happy!'

Clapping his hands together again, the kitchen seemed to fill with movement and life. Gas ignited, microwaves switched on, sausages started to sizzle. A radio started playing some heavy rock track from the eighties, to which Uncle Gus began to bellow along. Rufus lifted his head and gave a low, lonely howl—either in suffering or enjoyment, Lily was unsure—while Lily herself turned to what appeared to be a giant grill and wondered how on earth she was going to fry thirteen eggs all at the same time.

10

SPECIAL GUEST

DESPITE HER LOW EXPECTATIONS, BREAKFAST APPEARED to be a success. At least, to Lily's knowledge no one complained about eggs she was sure were half over done and half under. As Aunt Gert scooped them onto plates she paused at each, as though aware which customer would appreciate which.

When the last customer to finish got up and headed back to his room, Uncle Gus clapped his hands together again, causing a line of hanging antique mugs to shudder.

'Good work, everyone,' he said, then reached up and pulled off both his chef's hat and beard-net. Thick, curly hair sprung up as though desperate to escape, and his beard bounced down to touch his chest. It was grey more than brown these days, but Uncle Gus still looked like he'd got a sheep stuck on his head and had to burrow holes for his eyes, nose and mouth. Lily's dad, who was starting to go bald, had missed the bus when the family's hair had been dished out.

'Your dad was wrong,' Aunt Gert said, smiling up at Lily. 'You do know the right way round for a spatula.'

Lily grimaced. 'Did he tell you I don't know the difference between sugar and salt?'

Uncle Gus bellowed with a sudden hurricane of laughter. 'You're safe there,' he said. 'We let the customers deal with the condiments themselves.' Then, smiling—at least as far as Lily could tell—he added, 'How are you, dear? Your dad said you were having a bad run of things.'

Lily shrugged. 'Lost my car, my flat, my job and my fiancé in the space of a couple of days.'

Aunt Gert came up to Lily and cupped both her cheeks with hands that smelled of orange zest. With an intent look in her eyes that made Lily a little nervous, she said, 'Which of those do you miss the most?'

Lily couldn't help but smile. 'The car,' she said.

Uncle Gus bellowed with laughter again. Aunt Gert threw her hands up in the air fast enough to make Lily's cheeks smart, then cried, 'But of course!'

The two turned and shared a high five, Uncle Gus's hand dwarfing that of Aunt Gert's. Lily, watching them with increasing nervousness, couldn't quite decide whether she had wandered into a circus or a lunatic asylum.

After taking Aunt Gert's hand and giving her a quick pirouette, Uncle Gus's smile abruptly dropped. 'Right, back to business. Lily, your father told us that he thought it would be good for you to get a nice overview of how things work around here. Just for a bit of work experience.'

'He thinks that all I can do is push buttons and make conference calls,' Lily said.

Aunt Gert cocked her head. She pulled a pair of spectacles out of a breast pocket and arranged them on her nose before looking up at Lily. She looked a little like a wizened hen, her eyes narrowing behind the precariously placed spectacles which also made her nose appear thinner.

'Tell me, dear, what salary were you commanding where you only had to push buttons and make conference calls?'

'A hundred and twenty grand a year,' Lily said, feeling her cheeks redden.

'Oh Lord, we're in the wrong profession,' Aunt Gert said, throwing her arms up in the air again.

'Starting,' Lily added with a sheepish grin. 'Plus quarterly performance-based increases and bonuses. All in, closer to two hundred.'

'Gosh, no wonder your jeans look as expensive as my car,' Aunt Gert said.

Lily shrugged. 'A hundred quid. On sale.'

Uncle Gus chuckled. 'Well, don't you worry, dear, we'll clear the button pusher out of you in no time. We've got someone coming in about the blocked downstairs toilet in the afternoon, but we'll save you the upstairs. And then there's the changeovers. However—' he clapped his hands again, '—first, we've got her in the annexe to take care of.'

Uncle Gus and Aunt Gert both gave a dramatic 'Oooh,' as they turned to face each other.

'Her in the annexe?' Lily said, frowning.

'She requires her breakfast at nine-thirty sharp every morning,' Aunt Gert said.

'When the cycle path opened and tourists started piling in again, we decided to expand a little bit,' Uncle Gus said. 'We had the conservatory added, turned a couple of storerooms into guestrooms, and acquired the annexe.'

'The annexe,' Aunt Gert echoed, as though it were some secret chamber that required a password to enter.

'We also decided to take on permanent guests, if there were any such offers,' Uncle Gus said. 'Just as a kind of insurance policy to get us through the quiet months. And when Victoria asked, we agreed.'

'Victoria?'

'Victoria Borton,' Aunt Gert said. 'She's a writer.'

'A writer.' This time it was Uncle Gus's turn to echo.

'Quite a famous one, I believe.'

'A writer?'

'A writer. Ooooh.' This time, both echoed Lily.

'So all you have to do is take her breakfast down to her, wait around for half an hour, then bring the trays back.'

'Why do I have to wait around? Can't I pick them up later?'

Uncle Gus and Aunt Gert exchanged a glance.

'Ah, of course,' Uncle Gus said. 'She doesn't know about the annexe.'

'The annexe.'

Uncle Gus went out of the kitchen and through a door into a glass conservatory where tables were arranged around the windows. Some needed to be cleared: Lily guessed it would be one of her first jobs.

'We forgot to mention that the annexe is not exactly on site,' Uncle Gus said. 'In fact, it's a little off site.'

He opened the door and stepped out on to a patio surrounded by roses, his slippers padding on the paving stones. A cool breeze drifted in, bringing the scent of rain and wet flowers.

'It's down there,' Uncle Gus said, pointing down the Willow River valley. The cycle path quickly disappeared out of sight into the trees, with the river itself only occasionally visible where it widened briefly when the fields flattened a little. Perhaps two miles distant, the valley curved out of sight, taking the railway line and Willow River away towards Brentwell and then on to Exeter.

And there, just before the final curve, the roof of a building poked out of the trees.

'You don't mean—'

'On your bike,' Aunt Gert said.

'The old station building at Moor Cross,' Uncle Gus said. 'It had been derelict since the seventies, when that station officially closed. The council put it up for sale and we snapped it up.' He clicked meaty fingers together. 'It's now officially the Willow River Guesthouse Annexe. We put in six rooms, but Victoria Borton pays for the lot, so it's just her in there.'

'Not quite two hundred grand a year, but it's still a decent earner,' Aunt Gert said, giving Lily a wink.

'Which means we want to keep hold of her,' Uncle Gus said. 'And the first thing to do is make sure her breakfast isn't late.' He turned and nodded at a cuckoo clock on the conservatory wall. 'That old thing's five minutes fast, thank God, but you've only got ten minutes before she starts shouting. On your bike. Gert will bring out the hamper.'

'Literally on your bike,' Aunt Gert said. 'It's outside, by the back wall.'

'My shoes—'

'Better go and get them on.'

Lily dashed back through the guesthouse to the entrance, grabbed her shoes out of the rack and went out. It took a minute to get back around to the conservatory door due to a series of awkward flowerbeds, but by the time Lily had given up negotiating what she felt sure was Uncle Gus's attempt at a garden maze and vaulted over the last one, Aunt Gert was standing by the back door, a hamper sitting on an outside bench seat nearby, tapping her bare wrist.

'This is the real test of what you're made of,' she said. 'You've got nine minutes to get down that path and get that hamper to the door of Room Three. Can you make it? This is real pressure, Lily. None of your boardroom charades.'

Aunt Gert gave a little titter of a laugh which betrayed her own nervousness. Lily picked up the hamper and secured it to a rack over the bike's back wheel with a couple of hanging elastic fasteners.

'Go, Lily,' Aunt Gert said. 'And don't look back.'

Lily, who hadn't ridden a bike for more than ten years, felt gangly and awkward as she pushed the old grandma bike forward and climbed on to a seat that was too low for her. As her knees pumped nearly to her chin, she realised it had been set up for Aunt Gert's diminutive figure, but it was too late now. Steadying it as she took a bumpy paved path that led down to a gate opening out of the guesthouse's sloping gardens onto the cycle path, she stood up in the seat to make pedaling easier, picking her route over the larger of the stones.

At the gate she had to get off just long enough to open it, closing it again behind her as Aunt Gert called, 'Don't forget to close it! Sometimes that cheeky sod Donbury uses that path to move his cattle!'

Then she was moving along the smooth tarmac of the cycle path, aware, however, that the old station at Moor Cross was still some distance off.

Pressure was something Lily had come to take for granted working for Davidson's. The knowledge that as little as a smile in the wrong place or the stress placed on the wrong part of a sentence could cause the collapse of a multi-million pound deal had made her cool in difficult situations, but perhaps what Jonas Davidson had said was right: you couldn't take the countryside out of the bumpkin.

Time-keeping had never been her strong point, and even now, aware she had mere minutes to meet the nine-thirty deadline, she found herself slowing, wanting to take in the gorgeous river views, appreciate the freshness of the air, savour the seasonal turn as summer gave way to autumn. With the wind rustling the hanging willow branches as they trailed in the water, she felt like she was missing out by going too fast. Time seemed to slow, and by the time the old Moor Cross station building came into sight, now transformed into a pretty cottage, she was at least five minutes late.

Parking her bike, removing the straps from the hamper and carrying them up the steps and along the old platform —now dotted with flower boxes—to the entrance added another couple of minutes. By the time she was inside and had found her way to the door of Room Three— unhelpfully on the end of the upper floor past both Rooms Five and Six—she was at least ten minutes late.

The door flew open just as she was setting the hamper down.

'I'm sorry I'm late … I—'

The woman was huge and billowing, like a storm cloud dressed in a nightgown. Wild, grey-white hair cascaded over wide shoulders, and deep blue eyes glowered at Lily through nineteen-fifties horn-rims.

'Do you know the time?'

Lily grimaced. 'I'm sorry, I saw some swans—'

The woman frowned. 'Gertrude? Did you uncover a time machine? Or is it a new moisteriser? I must say, I saw one in a catalogue the other day and it was practically calling your name.'

'I'm Lily,' Lily said. 'I'm Angus and Gertrude's niece.'

'Oh. Getting a few hours in to pay for your studies?'

'I'm twenty-six.'

'Well, it's never too late to start. Wait downstairs, please. I do hope the fruit isn't too warm.'

'Well, it's a little chilly out—'

'And the sausage hasn't lost its crispness.'

'I don't know—'

'And if it's touching the beans, that'll be another black mark. How fast did you take those corners?'

'Pretty slow.'

'Well, maybe you'll be better than the part timer they had in last year. You know, there was one day the whole lot was slopped in against the clingfilm. I had words with your uncle and aunt after that, I'll say.'

'I'll do my best.'

'Well, wait downstairs please. All this idle chatter is eating into my breakfast time.'

As though having just made the joke of the century, the old woman burst into a flutter of laughter. Lily began to wonder if everyone associated with the Willow River Guesthouse was certifiably insane.

She was still wondering when Victoria Borton took the hamper inside and slammed the door in Lily's face.

'Hey....'

She could hear Victoria stomping away into her room, so she slouched back downstairs and sat outside on the old platform edge, enjoying the scenery as she waited. It was turning into a beautiful autumn day, the few clouds banished by a bright sun, a light tickle of breeze enough to keep her honest without wishing she'd brought a proper jacket. The trees alongside Willow River rustled in the breeze, and a cackle of ducks sounded from below the river bank.

'Girl!'

Lily was daydreaming when the cry from overhead shook her out of her reverie. She turned to see Victoria leaning out of an upstairs window, the hamper in her hands.

'No need to come back up. Can you catch?'

'Not very well—'

Too late, the hamper came sailing through the air. Lily reached out for it, half catching it before it slipped through her hands and thudded unceremoniously against the old platform. From inside came the crack of breaking crockery.

Feeling flustered, Lily looked up, ready to give the old woman a few choice words, but the window was already shut, the curtains drawn across.

Afraid of what Uncle Gus might say but at the same time not caring, she fixed the hamper back onto the bike and headed back to Willow River Guesthouse, wishing she'd had the opportunity to give Victoria Borton a piece of her mind.

11

WHISPERS OF FORGIVENESS

PETE HELD THE PHONE AGAINST HIS CHEST. 'IT'S UNCLE Gus for you,' he told Lily, who was brooding at the kitchen table with a glass of wine in front of her.

'I don't want to talk to him,' Lily said. 'I quit.'

'He says sorry for Mrs. Borton, but that the experience should be character building.'

'I don't care,' Lily said. 'I have my payoff. I don't need to deal with people like that. I can sit around for six months if I want. Maybe I'll go travelling.'

Pete leaned into the phone. 'She says she's rich, she doesn't need to deal with idiots, and she might go travelling.' Pete frowned, nodding. 'Uh huh. Right. Okay, got it.' He looked back at Lily. 'Uncle Gus wants to know what he needs to do to tempt you back. He says there's a large group coming in tomorrow and he thinks the egg count could go over twenty in a single go. You did such a good job with the thirteen you did this morning that unless he hires someone from the TV he can't possibly replace you. And the icing on the cake—or the salt on the eggs, if you like—is that he'll give you a pay rise. How does an extra twenty-five pence an hour sound?'

Lily couldn't help but smile. 'Twenty eggs, you say? Tell him to make it thirty-pence and I'll be there at seven o'clock. On one condition, though.'

'What?'

'I don't have to deliver to that old bag in the station house.'

Pete relayed the message into the phone.

'Alright, he said you've got a deal.'

Pete hung up and sat down at the table. 'Are you sure you're alright?'

'I just had a bad first day, that's all. After getting humiliated by that old woman, I had to scrub toilets, clean bins, and pick up some crusty old sock someone had left under a bed. I swear the thing moved when I touched it.'

Pete smiled. 'That's the hotel industry for you.'

'I'm earning eight pounds an hour to pick up other people's rubbish.'

'That's more than I was paying you, and don't forget, it's eight pounds thirty from tomorrow.'

'Wow, lucky me.'

'You know, when I was a kid, I helped out in that guesthouse for free. It was expected. By then, Gus was already running things as Gran and Grandad got too old, but I was there carrying out plates of beans on toast before school, then cutting the grass and emptying the bins after. It's not that hard, if you learn to appreciate it.'

'Do you think I'm weak?'

Pete leaned across and put a hand over Lily's. 'You're not weak, Lily. At least, not in some ways. You managed to channel all your energy and the brains you got from your mother's side into getting a First from Oxford and a top job in a London company. That's not bad, is it?'

'Not doing me much good now, is it?'

'You just have to work your way back up. And one way to do that, is to understand the foundations that your life is built on. Someone empties the bins in those ivory towers. Someone hoovers the carpets. And someone delivers the breakfasts to the lords in their castles. Put yourself in the shoes of those people for a while and you'll get a better perspective of things. You'll appreciate the view better the higher you climb, and you'll also understand how the people below you feel. Never take anything for granted, and don't be afraid of a bit of hard work. Just look at your mother. She makes all those things she sells in her shop for five quid a pop. She could order them in out of some factory in China if she wanted to, but she doesn't. She likes getting her hands dirty, because it makes the money that she earns feel deserved.'

'So you think I don't appreciate money?'

'All I think is that you shouldn't give up on the guesthouse after one day.'

Lily sighed. 'I'll do my best.'

'Try to look at it differently. You're not just there to pick up crusty socks and fry eggs. You're there to make people happy. To entertain them. And at the same time, you can learn from them in return. You're coming into contact with people from all over the place, from all different walks of life. Don't miss the opportunity to get to know them a little.'

Lily nodded.

'I'll try.'

Pete patted her hand. 'Good girl. Now, is there a beer in the fridge I can drink to accompany you and that wine?'

'I think so.' Lily held up the rest of the wine bottle. 'Should I save some for Mum?'

Pete shook his head. 'No, I think she's busy with

Doreen Volume 4. It arrived in the mail this morning. I think she's scared to turn it off in case Doreen finds out.'

'Well, I suppose if it makes her happy.'

'Oh, by the way, a letter came for you this morning.'

Pete headed to the fridge to get a beer, then picked an envelope up from a rack on the kitchen counter. He came back to the table and handed it to Lily.

'Anyone you know?'

The address was handwritten, the envelope adorned with painted swirls.

Steve.

She picked it up, turned it over, then forced a shrug. 'I'm not sure,' she said.

Half an hour later, after an increasingly forced conversation with her dad, she headed to her room, closed the door, and pulled the letter out of her pocket. She had been home a couple of weeks now and still not ventured back into the online world. Eventually Steve must have figured out where she had gone and hunted out her address.

Their entire relationship had taken place in London. Steve had met her parents just once, when they had visited London last year, but had otherwise shown no interest in visiting her hometown or learning about her background. She had existed only as London Lily, whereas, now that she thought about it, he had barely been more than Soho Steve. His parents were from Norfolk ... or was it Suffolk? His dad was a farmer, or a miner, perhaps. Lily could no longer remember. Caught up in big city living, Lily realised their relationship had built itself with none of the foundations her dad claimed were so important. Now, as she opened the letter, she felt like she was shaking up a box of old bones and preparing to dump them out all over the floor.

Dear Lily, it began, in a floral script which so reminded Lily of a wedding catalogue that it was like receiving an arrow to the heart.

I'm guessing that you don't want to talk to me right now. That's understandable. I made a few minor errors of judgement and now I'm suffering. Believe me, I'm suffering. I haven't painted a thing in two weeks. Not a thing. Can you imagine that? When I used to be so prolific? Honestly, your reaction to what was really just a misunderstanding cut a hole out of my soul and I doubt I'll ever fully recover. I've heard people say that they suffer for their art, but to this degree? I doubt it.

Anyway, I wanted to tell you that I still love you and forgive you for your overreaction. I realise I wasn't being fair in allowing you to fund my creative endeavours, but we did agree at the beginning of our relationship that we would support each other, didn't we? I was always there when you needed a shoulder to cry on, wasn't I? Don't try to say I wasn't there for you. I always was. And you used to be there for me. All it took was a little overreaction and a mistake and you've put my entire career in jeopardy. Shocking, isn't it? However, I do forgive you.

I still love you, Lily. Don't forget all those wonderful times we had together. Remember that time we sat by Tower Bridge and watched the sun go down? Or that time we had that picnic in Regent's Park when that goose stole our tuna sandwiches? Or that boat trip we took up the Thames last July? Come on, Lily, we had some great times together, and we could have more.

I've not quite got to the point where I'll be stalking you, haha), but you owe me an explanation. I've talked to some investors about covering the studio costs, so don't worry too much about that.

But my poor, poor broken heart, that should be your priority.

You don't have to write back to me, but I would at least

appreciate a liked post or a brief emoji comment somewhere, just to acknowledge that you've seen this letter.

Yours, with all my heart,

Steve xxx

She had to put a hand over her mouth to stop herself from screaming out loud. He had never been one for words; Steve's skill was with his hands, she remembered with no little fondness. However, despite the endearing awkwardness of his letter, a minor error of judgement had closed the door on their relationship for good.

It wasn't that he had subtly blamed her for ruining his career.

It wasn't that he had suggested she should start paying his rent, nor that he had accused her of overreacting to the presence of another woman in his studio.

It was that she had never, not once, set foot on a Thames riverboat.

She remembered sitting by Tower Bridge: it had been delightful, because some firework display had been going on in a park south of the river, lighting up the night sky, and she remembered the goose in Regent's Park, because shortly before it made off with a tuna sandwich, it had looked pretty keen on taking her nose. One day, she might look back on those days with something like nostalgia.

But she had never even liked the big old river that flowed through London. Willow River was plenty big enough for her liking, and she wasn't even a fan of crossing over the bridges in London. Something about the way the water swirled around the bridge supports, like a giant fluid beast, ready to swallow someone up.

Had he even suggested a river cruise, he would have needed to convince her, and she felt certain she would remember her reluctance had it come to a discussion. But she would most certainly have said no, and in the unlikely event she had said yes, she would have remembered every second of the trip, likely through a fear of an imminent death.

Whoever he had shared an intimate evening with on a Thames riverboat, it most certainly hadn't been her.

FRESH RESOLVE

'WE'RE PLEASED TO SEE YOU MADE IT BACK,' UNCLE GUS said, planting massive hands clad in comical pink gloves on his overlarge hips. 'We did wonder, but you've clearly got your mother's gumption. The good news is that a member of the group cancelled, so we're down to eighteen eggs.'

'And the bad?'

'Did I say there was bad?'

Lily cocked her head. 'There always is. Whenever someone says, "The good news" it always means there's bad news coming. So, what is it?'

Uncle Gus rolled his eyes and sighed. 'Well, if you must have it, your aunt got out of bed the wrong side this morning and banged her knee on the bedside table, right on the corner. She's able to hobble about and fulfil most of her duties, but I'm afraid cycling is out. So you're on Victoria Borton duty again, I'm afraid.'

'That was one of my conditions about coming back.'

Uncle Gus spread his hands. 'Oh, Lillian, dear. Be a team player. You're family, after all. And can you really see me on a bike?'

'What about Dave, the kid you've got cutting the grass?'

'The student?' Uncle Gus shook his head. 'He's cross-eyed. He'd end up in the river. And plus, he only comes in at eleven o'clock.'

'What about Mavis, the lady who makes up the bedrooms?'

'We sent her once and they fell out. They got into a fist fight.'

'Seriously?'

'No. But she has a dodgy hip. Plus, she's employed as a cleaner. You're employed as a general dogsbody.'

'Lucky me.'

'Pretty please?'

'I reserve the right to get into a fist fight with Victoria too, if she's rude or difficult.'

'Sure. As long as she doesn't leave, anything's fine.'

Despite her reluctance to visit the old lady, it was another fine autumn morning when she set out, riding along the river, this time making sure to give herself a few minutes of dithering time in case she came across any swans or other interesting birds. This morning, though, there was only a group of schoolboys on a canoeing trip, to whom she gave a cheerful wave, and a couple of early morning fishermen casting their lines into the dark waters underneath the riverbanks.

The more she thought about it, the fabled Willow River Guesthouse Annexe had proved a shrewd buy for Uncle Gus. Set in its own grounds, it would have made a beautiful country home in its own right. Lily wondered about turning the ground floor into some kind of café or restaurant, since the old platform was already set up as a useful outdoor terrace. Perhaps she could put the idea to Uncle Gus. It might even be nice to work there—

What are you doing? You're back for a breather, not permanently.

The voice of reason didn't sound very reasonable. The cool autumn days would soon give way to a far colder and rainier winter, the days short and the nights long, the town empty, and nothing much to do but sit around and watch TV.

A couple of sporty cyclists passed her, giving her a brief nod of acknowledgement as she pulled in to let them race past. Things had changed. Under the water, Willow River might still be the place where she had grown up, but above the water, it was greatly different. The summer no longer signaled the end of days, the beginning of ten months of bleakness. The autumn days were taking on a life of their own.

She was five minutes early when she knocked on Victoria's door.

'Who is it?' came a booming voice from inside.

'It's me, the same girl as yesterday,' Lily called. 'My name's Lily Markham, in case you were wondering.'

The door swung open, and Victoria stood there. While not quite the Mrs. Havisham she might have been, in a black evening dress adorned with a fur jacket, Victoria's appearance came as something of a surprise, particularly as it was not yet nine-thirty in the morning. Lily caught a strong whiff of perfume and took a step back.

'I wasn't wondering,' Victoria said. 'But perhaps I'll jot it down. I may include you in a book, however I can't guarantee you'll make it to the end.'

'That's too bad,' Lily said. 'Particularly after I included an extra sausage.'

'Are you concerned that I am underweight?'

'I grilled them extra lean.'

'So you've been upgraded from delivery person to chef?'

'My aunt hurt her knee falling out of bed, so I said I'd take over.'

'Falling out of bed….' Victoria frowned as she stared up at the ceiling, making a mental note. 'An interesting way to die….'

'Or just to hurt one's knee.'

'Yes, yes. Well, anyway, you may wait downstairs, Felicity.'

'Lily. My name is Lily.'

'That's nice. I'm sure it is.'

Victoria snatched the hamper out of Lily's hands and shut the door in her face. Lily stared at the varnished pine for a couple of seconds, then let out a sigh and headed downstairs. This time, to avoid breaking any more plates, she took a seat in a small common room, which would once have been the old station's waiting area. A television stood in a corner, a shelf of books and DVDs beside it. Framed pictures of the old station—some in black and white—some in colour, hung from the walls. Through the rear window was a little car park, beside it a grassy area that had been roughly cut. Lily was wistfully imagining it full of picnic benches, flowerbeds, and children's play equipment, when a voice came shuddering down from upstairs.

'Felicity? Where are you?'

Lily let out a sigh and headed upstairs. Victoria Borton was standing in the hallway, her bizarre outfit now adorned with a wide-brimmed hat, a single black rose pocking through a ribbon.

'I thought you might have done the unthinkable and left,' Victoria said.

'No, I'm still here. And it's Lily.'

'No, it's a rose,' Victoria said, reaching up and touching the flower in her hat, before letting out a barrage of laughter which made Lily frown. 'I painted it black, just for effect.'

'If you don't mind me asking, why are you dressed like Cruella de Vil?'

Victoria laughed again. 'Quite observant of you, dear, although you're a little misplaced with your assessment. I do appear quite the femme fatale, do I not?'

'I'd be scared enough to run away if I wasn't charged with collecting your breakfast things,' Lily said.

'Exquisite!' Victoria cried, throwing her hands up in the air. 'I need to get this down. Mandy, you may leave.'

'Lily!'

'Yes, yes, that works too.'

Victoria bustled back into the room and slammed the door. Lily, giving a bemused shake of her head, retrieved the hamper and headed back downstairs.

Aware she was on a free run for time, she fixed the hamper to the bike then decided to walk it back instead, allowing herself to flush the crazy old woman out of her mind, and to let the calming, peaceful nature back in. She found herself thinking of London, of whether or not she would respond to Steve, what she might say, even what she might do from here.

While London living and supporting Steve in his creative endeavours had taken a chunk out of her salary, she still had plenty left, and the idea of investing in a little café or tearoom in the peaceful surrounds of Willow River was something she couldn't quite shake out of her mind. Having a borderline nutjob living upstairs might not work out quite so well, though.

Back at the guesthouse, Uncle Gus had left her a note

pinned up in the kitchen, listingthe day's jobs. He had apparently taken Aunt Gert to hospital to have her knee checked, meaning Lily, on only her second full day, had been left in charge.

If that was the case, perhaps she could allow herself a manager's cup of coffee. There was some in a filter leftover from breakfast, so she reheated it in a microwave and wandered through to the little reception desk near the front entrance. She found a bell and a logbook of current and expected guests, as well as a computer. She switched it on, fully expecting it to require a password, but was surprised to find it went straight to a home screen, the icons set against a pretty wallpaper picture of the bridge across Willow River further up the valley. She hadn't been online since fleeing London, but the internet icon beckoned her.

Feeling a sense of trepidation, she gave it a little click.

Her old social media accounts were still there, and Lily felt a little disappointed that so little had changed. Sure, there was a long list of the updates she would have previously cleared daily—or several times daily, if she were honest about it—but she was dismayed how little of it was of any relevance. There were a few interesting updates from her old work colleagues—one had been transferred to Spain, and another had—to Lily's frustration—been promoted into Lily's old position—but most were the same inane entries as before. Complaints about this and that, vague fishing posts inciting questions, pictures of food, small children, cats, shared memes or humourous photo galleries she had seen hundreds of times before, and all manner of other pointless stuff she now realised she had been happily living without.

Her email was slightly more interesting, with messages from her landlord, Steve's landlord, the council, and Davidsons' HR department. She was officially unemployed, homeless, but was no longer paying for Steve's studio. There was also an email from the car garage, asking if she ever planned to pick up her newly repaired car. She sent a quick message back, asking them to sell it, and if they wanted to give her a share, to donate the money to a charity instead.

She also had a couple of job interview requests, much to her surprise after the hurry she had been in to apply. One was from a company that three months ago she would have jumped at the chance to work for, but after just two days of cycling along Willow River, she felt reluctant to swap the trees and fresh air for the glass and chrome of another tower block office. She replied, thanking them for the opportunity but saying that she had decided to take a bit of a sabbatical.

She was about to log off, when she found her fingers hovering over keys she would have once been excited to press.

Don't do it, a little voice whispered.

She did it anyway, bringing up Instagram and pulling up Steve's page. In the past it had featured endless shots of his current projects, and the growing number of his followers had actually made Lily a little jealous. However, she had been tempered by the occasional posts featuring herself, mentioned as his girlfriend and latterly as his wife-to-be, all of which had received significant interest and likes, as well as lots of nice comments. There had been a few bad ones—Steve was quite the hot property among young artists, much to Lily's frustration—but Steve had been quick to delete anything too trolling.

Now, however, the first picture that came up was a shot of a new studio, with a beaming Steve standing extremely close to the woman Lily had seen in his old one. So close, that even by zooming in the picture, she couldn't see any daylight between them, and one of his arms was suspiciously behind her, possibly around her back. Due to the lighting in that section of the picture, Lily couldn't be a hundred percent sure.

In a new studio, with a new sponsor!—the caption read.

The comments were going off. *New girlfriend? What a beautiful couple! I hope she's not distracting you from painting! Hot stuff!*

Steve had declined to reply to any of the posts, but Lily found herself scrolling through lists of likes, looking for any from Steve, or other accounts belonging to people she had once considered friends.

Her eyes were beginning to hurt before she realised how ridiculous she was being. She checked the posting date on the picture, and saw it was several days after the postmark on the letter she had received. Without a reply, perhaps Steve had moved on.

A chasm seemed to open up beneath her feet, and Lily felt her emotions draining away. Until now she had felt in control: all she had to do was reply and everything would be all right. Give it a little time for her anger to fade and for Steve to learn his lesson, and they'd be back on again. She still loved him, after all, and they had been due to marry next year.

Now, those lingering dreams felt crushed like a rotten lemon under her feet.

She almost fell off the chair when the bell over the front door pinged and a couple of people entered. Both women in their thirties, they had a nervous look about them. One had her hair tied back underneath a floppy hat, and wore a green Montbell rain jacket zipped up to her neck as though she had just returned from a moorland hike. The other wore a woolly hat with an orange bobble and spectacles, over a black sweater and jeans. She was clutching something to her chest, and Lily glanced at it, wondering if they belonged to that increasingly rare breed: female train enthusiasts. She was about to point out that the train had stopped running along this section of line several years ago, when the woman shifted and a familiar name became visible along the book's top edge.

'Are you … are you looking for a room?' Lily asked.

The two women exchanged a nervous glance, then the closest—Bobble Hat—looked back and shook her head.

'No, no, I mean, we might be, depending … we were wondering if Victoria Borton is staying here. We're … old friends.'

The woman had shifted again, the book's cover no longer visible. Instinctively Lily knew these were fans of the writer holed up in the guesthouse's annexe, and remembered how she had reacted once to someone interrupting her and Steve at a restaurant to tell him how much his art was loved. That the crazed fan—as Lily considered it—was an attractive girl no older than nineteen or twenty, had made it even worse.

It was doubtful either of these two Anoraks had any intention of sleeping with Victoria, but stalking her definitely wasn't out of the question. Lily found herself shaking her head.

'I'm sorry, we're fully booked at the moment, but none of our guests have that name.'

The two women glanced at each other, and a strange sound came from each at the same time. It was a kind of whisper made without really moving their mouths, the sort you might make while trying to talk during a class at school without being caught. It took Lily a moment to figure out what there were saying, but they helpfully repeated the same phrase several times, as though excited.

'Assumed name … assumed name….'

Bobble-Hat lifted the book and turned it over. Lily found herself looking at a picture of a much younger, thinner, and thoroughly airbrushed Victoria, the kind of author picture where the subject is staring at the camera with a strong, confident gaze, yet still an air of mystery, as though they know the answers to everything but are refusing to tell. She wondered if professional photographers had filters or templates labeled "all-knowing author".

'Um, this lady,' Bobble-Hat said. 'We're old friends.'

'Family … we're family,' muttered Zip-Up, in that same whisper-talk as before. Lily imagined sharing a conversation was a nightmare for these two anywhere more public than a library.

Lily shook her head. 'I'm sorry, I've not seen her before.'

The two looked crestfallen. In a way it wasn't a lie; the woman occupying the annexe looked nothing like the woman in the picture. A vague resemblance, but that was all.

Zip-Up and Bobble-Hat looked at each other again, shared some snippet of information that this time Lily couldn't catch, then turned to leave.

Realising they were about to go, something Lily had learned in a business class kicked in: never miss an opportunity for a sale.

'Muffin?' she said, reaching into a basket on the counter and picking up one of Aunt Gert's homemade strawberry muffins, wrapped haphazardly in cling-film. 'Two for the price of one. Today only.'

The two women muttered something again, then both gave a collective shake of their heads as though they were really one organism rather than two, and then went out.

OLIVE BRANCH

'SO … WHAT'S THE DEAL WITH THAT WOMAN IN THE annexe up there at the guesthouse?' Lily asked, sitting on an old chair in their garage as she watched her dad glue pieces of coloured glass to a large piece of plywood leaning against the wall.

'You mean Victoria Borton?'

'Yes. I had a couple of people show up today, asking for her.'

'She's quite the celebrity, according to Gus. Did you look her up online?'

'I had a look, but it seems like she's written about a hundred books, so I got kind of lost. All romantic type stuff. I suppose she must be pretty popular, but I had a look at her rankings, and none of them were especially impressive.'

'It was one book that did it,' Pete said. 'Gosh, it was a few years back now. Must have been when you were at university, so you were probably drinking your way through everything and missed all the hype.'

'I didn't drink that much,' Lily protested, remembering

long, wild nights in Oxford's scattering of nightclubs, all day drinking sessions and banging lines of vodka or tequila before heading for packed dance floors.

Pete chuckled and rolled his eyes, as if to say, *I know.* 'She had this one book that hit all the bestseller lists, got on the TV and everything. I have a feeling they made a movie out of it, but I don't remember. It's probably on every Christmas, something like that.'

'What was it? Do you remember the title?'

'Yeah. "*The Trainspotter's Guide to Romance.*" It was one of those Richard Harris-type rom-coms.'

'Richard Curtis.'

Pete grinned. 'Yeah, one of his, too. I imagine Hugh Grant was in it, or Colin Firth. In fact, your mother almost certainly has it on DVD somewhere. Anyway, for about a year, it was absolutely huge. Kind of like *Bridget Jones's Diary* for complete outcasts, not just pretty girls pretending to not be pretty.'

'So, she's a bit of a star, then?'

'That's the funny thing. She absolutely was, and she had a ton of books out beforehand, so a few of them got popular too, but since *The Trainspotter's Guide to Romance* came out, she hasn't published anything. We obviously thought nothing of it, until she went and moved into the annexe two years ago. Gus is convinced she's hiding in there now trying to write some masterpiece of a follow up.'

'It's quite exciting really, isn't it?'

'It's a little bit complex. Gus obviously doesn't want her to leave because she's paying a small fortune, but at the same time, her fans are starting to home in on her, because he told me random nerds are showing up every week or two now. Luckily, none of them know about the annexe, because the rooms are no longer advertised. So, for now she's safe, but if they find out … she'll probably have to move on.'

Lily mulled this all over while she went back into the house, leaving her dad to finish his latest project. Mum had gone out to a board game night at a friend's house, and with nothing else to do, Lily squatted by her parents' DVD cabinet, and there, sure enough, was a copy of *The Trainspotter's Guide to Romance*.

One hundred minutes and a bottle of wine later, Lily found herself wiping her eyes while at the same time rubbing her cheeks, aching from the constant laughter.

In the movie, a hopeless twenty-something trainspotter —rejected by her own community for being a girl—falls in love with a handsome train conductor along a stretch of line about to be closed down. After many adventures, farcical situations, and stupid, so-bad-they're-good jokes, not to mention a couple of proper tear-jerker scenes, the two main characters end up married, buying an old station building, and turning it into a bakery. She turns out to be more attractive than at first appeared, while he is revealed to have numerous nerdy pursuits such as jam-making and embroidery. The movie's tagline, "When is a train, not a train?", stayed on Lily's mind long after she'd turned off the TV and retired to bed.

The "answer"—somewhat forced in Lily's opinion— was revealed in a voiceover at the end of the movie, when the main characters share a smile before delivering a tray of high-calorie chocolate-filled muffins to a family sitting on a table outside, the woman gently touching a pregnancy bump as she looks at the man: "When it's a fresh start."

It didn't have any of the catchiness that Lily might have considered for a potentially successful advertising campaign, but it had clearly worked. The parallels of Victoria being holed up in just such a converted station building hadn't been lost on Lily, however, nor that she had briefly imagined turning the station into some kind of restaurant or café, almost exactly as had happened at the movie's conclusion. Perhaps the movie had some kind of universal appeal, and Lily, who had felt enough moments of déjà vu to suggest she might have seen it before, perhaps on some drunken night at university, wondered if its overarching theme and meaning had slipped into a collective consciousness.

Whatever the truth was, she felt certain that Victoria, perhaps in her wisdom, or perhaps not, had holed herself up at the fictional end of her own story in order to try to write a sequel.

Clouds spotted the sky the next morning, and Lily took an umbrella with her as she rode out to the annexe, just in case. With Aunt Gert rather shockingly now in a plaster cast—Lily had initially assumed the fall was a ruse to cajole her into making the annexe delivery—Lily had no choice but to take on more kitchen duties. With Uncle Gus humming along to a tune on the radio, and Aunt Gert giving directions from a chair in the corner, Lily fried eggs, grilled bacon, stirred beans, toasted bread, chopped mushrooms, and arranged bread rolls into wicker baskets with a speed and robotic efficiency that made a mockery of her two days on the job. When it came to preparing Victoria's hamper, however—essentially a large plate of fried food all held in place by a generous helping of cling-film—Lily decided to take a different tack. She allowed the sausages and beans—although she gave the sausages a squeeze in some kitchen tissue to soak up a bit of the fat, but instead of the bacon and fried mushrooms, she added a side salad and a bowl of fruit, and also included a mini-box of bran flakes and a small carton of milk. While the author photo had obviously been studio enhanced, it was quite clear that Victoria had put on a bit of weight during the intervening years, and if Lily was going to be responsible for delivering the woman's breakfast, she felt it necessary to introduce both a little variation and some vitamins.

And just to make sure Victoria finished everything, Lily wrote down a joke she had heard on the internet recently and slipped the piece of paper on top of the hamper. Before serving the food, she taped the answer to the plate's bottom.

She whistled as she rode along the cycle path. A couple of fishermen whom had already become familiar gave her a wave, and not far from the annexe an older gentleman walking a dog gave her a kind smile. The leaves of the willows were starting to change colour, and the breeze was getting colder. Soon she would need to start wearing a hat or jacket, but Lily couldn't remember the last time she had felt happier. The hamper on the back of the bike, which both Uncle Gus and Aunt Gert had worried about, felt like a true purpose. Only time would tell whether it would make her—and the entire guesthouse—crash and burn, but she turned on enough charm to convince her aunt and uncle that she knew what she was doing.

As she climbed the stairs to the upper floor, however, the doubts began to creep in. What if Victoria threw a tantrum and decided to leave? Uncle Gus's business would take a real hit, and Lily would possibly need to start job hunting all over again.

Her hand shook as she knocked on the door.

'Mandy? Is that you?'

'Yes, it's me, Lily,' Lily called through the door. 'Breakfast delivery.'

The door flew open, and Victoria stood there, flamboyantly dressed in a floral sweater over a long, ankle-length skirt. One half of her hair was in rollers, the other half hanging straight to her shoulder. Victoria was yet to apply makeup, and looked every bit of her fifty-something years, her eyes a little gummy as though she'd been on the wine, her skin a little puffy. Under her eyes, liver spots had begun to appear from beneath yesterday's peeling concealer.

'Ah, Mandy, you're fifteen minutes early.'

'Twelve. And it's Lily. I felt certain you would want to get breakfast over with in order to enjoy the rest of the day.'

'What's got you so chirpy this morning?'

Lily couldn't help but grin. 'I'm afraid there have been a couple of alterations to the menu. I hope you'll be forgiving … because forgiveness is an art form not often studied in itself.'

She wondered whether Victoria would spot the quote lifted straight from the movie made of her book. The older woman cocked her head a little, cleared her throat, and reached out for the hamper.

'Yes, well, that may be so. I suppose I'll have to see what alterations you've made, first.'

'I'm thinking only of you,' Lily said.

'Well, that's good, because I don't do tips,' Victoria said. 'Something of a personal rule.'

'A noble one,' Lily said. 'Should I wait downstairs as usual?'

'Wait a moment.'

Victoria set down the hamper and lifted the whicker

lid. Lily watched as the old woman crinkled her nose and frowned.

'Well, I've eaten worse at conventions, although forfeiting the bacon … shame on you … what's this?'

She picked up the piece of paper.

'It's an important question you're going to need the answer for,' Lily said.

'"When is a sparrow not a sparrow?" What on earth do you mean?'

Before Lily could answer, Victoria turned over the paper. 'Oh, I see. The answer is taped to the bottom of the plate. So what you're trying to say is that I need to eat all this … green stuff … in order to answer this existential question?'

Lily nodded.

'A tricky little thing, aren't you? Have you ever considered writing a book? You'd probably be quite suited to the mystery genre.'

'No, I haven't.'

'Well, perhaps you should try. Can't be a waitress forever, can you?'

Lily grimaced. 'Maybe I'll take your advice. I'll borrow a few post-its from reception and start scribbling on my breaks.'

'They give you breaks? Luxury, I'll say. When I was working in the coal refinery, we got one break at noon to shake the dust out of our boots.'

Lily didn't remember anything about working in a coal refinery on Victoria's Wikipedia page. While it was possible she had done some part time work in her youth, Lily felt it more likely that her isolation had left her one squirt of mustard short of a decent hotdog.

'I'll wait downstairs,' she said.

Thirty minutes later, she was still waiting. Victoria had never taken so long to eat before, so as the cuckoo clock on the conservatory wall announced ten o'clock, she headed back upstairs and gave a light tap on the door.

'Ms Borton? Sorry to bother you, but are you all right in there?'

No response came. Lily waited a couple of minutes, then gave another light tap. Still no response. A little fearful now that something might have happened to Victoria, she tried the door and found it unlocked. Gently pushing the door open, she stepped inside.

'Victoria?'

Uncle Gus had told her this was a suite, and it felt like entering a flat rather than a hotel room. A little hall lay in front of her, a bathroom to one side, a small kitchen to the other. Ahead was a closed door.

Lily took a few steps forward. The door, on an automatic spring, bumped closed behind her, making her jump, leaving her alone in the hall. She glanced into the kitchen, but it looked largely unused. A pot of coffee stood half empty, and a couple of large loaves of bread made by Aunt Gert and sold in the guesthouse's small shop suggested how Victoria kept herself alive for the rest of the day.

'Victoria?'

Lily crept down the hall to the closed door, listening for any sound of the reclusive writer. Only as she leaned against the door did she hear a kind of rapid gasping coming from inside.

Lily frowned. She really hoped Victoria was doing some kind of exercise, and not something a little more … private, maybe with another person she'd sneaked into her room. On the other hand, she could be lying on the ground, having a seizure or a stroke.

Just in case, Lily had no choice. She took a deep breath, gripped the door handle, and opened the door.

The room was a mess, clothes strewn everywhere, personal objects scattered across the floor. Under the chaos was a sofa to one side and a bed to the other, with a nice view from the window that looked out over the fields behind the old station. In front of the window, leaning over a desk, was Victoria, gasping and panting as she battered away on an old laptop computer.

'Oh, so sorry—'

Lily started to back away. Victoria turned. Her face was literally dripping with sweat which flew all over the floor as she continued to type while grinning wildly up at Lily.

'Rebecca, dear, what a star you are. Who'd have thought it? When is a sparrow not a sparrow? When it's asparagus. What a perfect, perfect opening line. Eight years I've been waiting for this lightning strike. I've got an opening, I've got a tone. I need a character. Come on, Rebecca, give me more, dear. Quickly! Give me more!'

'Ah … a girl? She's late for work, and she … ah … gets fired?'

'Perfect! More!'

'She … ah … goes to see her fiancé, but he's got another woman there, and she's … heartbroken.'

'What does he do? Some kind of office type?'

'What? Ah, no, he's an artist.'

'Perfect! The misstep! You're a natural. More! What does she do?'

'She runs. She runs away from her old life, back to her parents' place. And there … she's at a loose end … and she needs something to do, so she gets a job in her uncle's guesthouse. And there—'

'Yes, yes! What's our hook?'

Lily couldn't help but smile. 'She meets a crazy old writer who can't write anymore because her last book was too successful. And they … help each other.'

'Genius. Go, Rebecca, get out. I can run with this. Come back tomorrow.'

As Victoria leaned over the computer, Lily spotted the hamper lying by the door. The food had been finished, the plate she had taped the joke's punchline to still turned upside down. The paper had gone, but as she glanced back at Victoria, she spotted it: taped to the top corner of Victoria's computer.

'Wait!' Victoria lifted a hand as Lily retrieved the hamper and started to back through the door. 'Who is she? What's her name?'

Lily smiled. 'Lily,' she said, unable to resist. 'Lily Markham.'

14

HISTORY

It felt weird knowing she might end up as a character in a book. Everything felt a little surreal as Lily pushed the bike back along the cycle path, pausing frequently to watch the ducks circling in the water. The spectre of her old life seemed suddenly so far away as she hummed a song she had heard this morning on Uncle Gus's radio. Perhaps she could dictate to Victoria how she wanted her life to go, and it would turn out that way in real life. She would meet a handsome man who wasn't a cheater or a sponge. To hell with it, he was actually a prince. And she would be his princess. Why not?

The sky had begun to cloud over as she reached the guesthouse, the first few fat drops of an oncoming shower falling around her as she hurried up the path, parked the bike, and headed inside. On the other hand, Victoria might have given up by tomorrow. After all, it had been eight years since her last book.

By the time Lily had washed the hamper's contents and set them to dry on a rack beside the sink, the windows of the conservatory were streaked with rain. Uncle Gus had taped a list of jobs to be done, but the large party staying overnight had left, and there were only two rooms still occupied. Lily had the next couple of days off, her schedule focused around the weekends, when the guesthouse was busier.

When she came back downstairs after finishing making up the second room, Uncle Gus and Aunt Gert were sitting in the dining area, hunched over a Scrabble board.

'Superficial,' Uncle Gus said with a triumphant grin. 'Thirty-seven.'

Aunt Gert sighed. 'I knew I should have got the plunger out when you swallowed that dictionary, instead of letting it digest. Fox. Nine.'

'I'll up your handicap to fifty tomorrow,' Uncle Gus said. 'Remedial. Oh, triple word score. Bing bong.'

'Lily? Do you know any decent nine letter words?'

Lily frowned. 'Impossible?' She counted on her fingers. 'Oh, that's ten.' Then, with a laugh, she added, 'No wonder the finance industry didn't work out.'

'Well, you're becoming an expert at changing beds, dear,' Aunt Gert said, then hunched back over the game as though the conversation was over.

Unsure quite what she should be doing for the remainder of her shift, Lily wandered through to the lobby, admiring the displays of antiques she had previously been too busy to enjoy. Her grandfather really had been a collector. She wondered if there was anything especially valuable hidden among all the ancient toys, fixtures, paintings, crockery, and appliances. A rare toaster from the fifties, perhaps? Or an old Victorian era spoon once licked by Prince Albert?

Through a door to the lobby's left was the guesthouse's little shop. Unmanned, customers had to ring a bell for assistance. About the size of a walk-in closet, about half was set aside for postcards, local guidebooks and pamphlets, and locally made crafts and foodstuffs. The other half was restored antiques, secondhand books, and old magazines. In one corner was another shelf labeled BRING ONE, TAKE ONE, a lending library of sorts for guests. On a bottom shelf, Lily was surprised to find a stack of old local newspapers, some dating back as far as the nineties, their corners starting to brown with age. She grabbed a handful, went back into the kitchens and made a coffee, then sat down on a sofa in the common area to have a look through.

The dates were all a bit random, with the first from January 1990, with the most recent dated last summer. At first Lily wasn't sure what connection they might have, until she turned to page five of one and found an article on the guesthouse.

Willow River Guesthouse receives top award

Family Magazine, Britain's leading national magazine for family welfare yesterday awarded Willow River Guesthouse of Willow River, Devon with first place in its Best for Families 1997 awards.

"I'm delighted," said the owner, Robert Markham, a longtime Willow River resident. "This is what our guesthouse is all about; providing a happy environment for families."

Underneath was a picture of Lily's grandfather, his face stoic as he held up a plaque, the picture too grainy to reveal its inscription. Her grandmother, Margaret, stood beside him, a wide grin on her face. To either side stood two young men, one rotund and bushy-haired, the other thinner and already balding. On Pete's left stood a much younger, slimmer, and less flamboyant version of her mother, a baby held in her arms.

Lily stared. That had to be her at roughly a year old. She smiled. Her first appearance in the press.

She got up and wandered through to the reception lobby, where she found the award, now collecting dust behind a pot of dusty plastic flowers. She gave it a quick polish with her sleeve and adjusted its position so that it was more visible to customers. Twenty-five years old it might be, but it was still something to be proud of.

Uncle Gus and Aunt Gert were still hunched over their Scrabble game, chuckling and muttering to each other, as rain now hammered against the windows. Lily, feeling happily invisible, refilled her coffee and went back to her sofa.

She soon discovered that the common theme the papers shared was that each had an article about the guesthouse. There were one or two more awards, then some special events, such as the hosting of a duck race down Willow River, a charity fete held in the gardens, and a visit from Prince Charles and the Duchess of Cornwall. Then there were a couple of offbeat ones, such as a carrier pigeon that had somehow ended up stuck in the conservatory with a message taped to its foot for a Scottish lord, and another as the starting point for an attempt by a local man to walk all the major railway lines in the United Kingdom while dressed as King Arthur. Dated 2002, shortly before the line had closed, a colour picture underneath the short article showed a grinning man in a cloak and crown holding a wooden sword aloft, standing beside her grandfather, a look of bemusement on his face.

Lastly, were the anniversary articles. These were easy to spot because they came every five years. In 1995 the guesthouse had celebrated forty years with a half-page picture taken from an upper floor of a group of people waving from a larger patio where the conservatory now stood. Aside from her grandparents, Uncle Gus and her dad, the picture was too grainy to reveal the identities of the other people in the group, although according to the caption, one of them was Phillip Schofield, come down from the BBC to make a speech at the party.

Ten years later, for the fiftieth anniversary, the picture was in colour and much clearer, the group this time standing at the front of the guesthouse. Lily felt a pang of regret that her grandmother was no longer there, and her grandfather seemed to have aged remarkably since the previous occasion. Uncle Gus had begun to take on his current appearance, his features mostly hidden by beard—albeit with less streaks of grey—and Aunt Gert was grinning as she leaned on his shoulder. Her own parents stood looking respectfully at the camera, with Lily standing to her mother's left, nine years old, gangly and dorky, her hair an awkward bob. She didn't remember the event, but she remembered hating that hair, growing it out and wearing it in a ponytail for years, until friends at university had convinced her to experiment more.

Of the other people in the picture, she recognised a couple: Martin Donbury, Jimmy's dad, stood beside her grandfather in a suit, and Lily vaguely remembered him once chairing the village council. Mary, her best friend at the time, was there to one side, standing next to her mother wearing a maid's apron. Lily briefly raised an eyebrow, having not known Mary's mother had once worked for Gus. She had always thought she worked in a florist's on the road between Willow River and Brentwell, but supposed she may have had more than one part time job.

Of greatest interest, however, was the woman standing beside her own mother. Not especially tall but with a presence that seemed to fill the picture, a younger, slimmer, and strikingly attractive version of Victoria Borton stared confidently into the camera. In a long purple dress with a white sash and a leopard print shawl, she looked like a movie star. One arm was hooked into her hip as though to execute a textbook photographer's pose, while the other held the hand of a little boy.

And in his other hand, he held Lily's.

They were about the same height. The boy, his hair close cropped, his ears sticking out a little awkwardly due to the oversized spectacles he wore, was the only one not looking at the camera. Instead, his head was tilted slightly and the smile he wore was directed solely at Lily.

She found herself smiling too. So, Victoria's connection with the Willow River Guesthouse ran deeper than her current use for it as a refuge. She had been staying here on the day of its fiftieth anniversary, travelling with a boy who had to be her son, even if he shared none of her flamboyance. And the boy, judging by the captured moment of time, had had a crush on Lily.

She wondered what had become of him. In her few brief minutes in Victoria's room she had seen no personal photos, and had found no other pictures—nor indeed a mention of him—during her search online.

A sudden bloom of heat into her cheeks came with the idea that he might be dead. Letting her rapidly beating heart gradually slow, she reasoned that while it was possible, it was only one of many possibilities. He looked about her age. Most likely he worked in a bank or some other office now, keeping his head down to avoid being recognised as the son of a famous writer. Perhaps he even had a family, a couple of kids.

She studied the photograph for a little longer, then carefully returned the newspapers to where she had found them. In the restaurant, Uncle Gus and Aunt Gert had finished their game of Scrabble and were shuffling a set of playing cards.

'Poker for matchsticks,' Aunt Gert said, holding up a huge bag of little sticks. 'You in?'

Lily pulled up a chair and sat down. 'Can I ask you guys something?'

'Sure,' Aunt Gert said.

'Depending on whether it's a trade secret or not,' Uncle Gus said. 'But in case you were wondering, no, I don't use hairspray.'

'Glad to have finally cleared that one up,' Lily said with a smile. 'It was about Victoria. I just wondered how long she's been staying here.'

Uncle Gus and Aunt Gert shared a glance. 'I could check the books,' Uncle Gus said. 'But off the top of my head, I'd say it's about three years.'

'But that's not her first time to stay, is it? She's stayed here a few times, hasn't she? I found a picture in an old newspaper.'

'She was a regular for years,' Uncle Gus said. 'Once or twice a year she'd show up for a couple of days. I believe she used to come here with her family when she was a child, way back when it first opened, when I was just a nipper.' He laughed. 'We used to play kiss chase out in the car park.' At Aunt Gert's glare, he added, 'I used to run like hell to get away from her.'

'And she had a little boy?'

'Michael. Yeah, nice lad. Quiet. Liked watching the trains. Lost interest a little when the line closed. I think the last time we saw him he must have been thirteen or fourteen. Probably busy with school, or with his dad.'

'Was Victoria married?'

'Not that we ever knew,' Aunt Gert said. 'She never stayed here with a man.'

'And her son never visits her now?'

Aunt Gert shook her head. 'No one comes to see her except a few of those weirdo fans of hers. The trainspotter types.'

Uncle Gus let out a loud cackle. 'Must be quite the paradox for her, all glammed up and that, getting hunted down by all these bookworms in orange anoraks. Right, who's dealing?'

Lily stuck up a hand. 'Me. I've got a feeling my luck is about to turn.'

15

PREDICTIONS AND SECRETS

THE RAIN DECIDED TO CLOSE IN OVER HER DAYS OFF, SO Lily spent most of her time at home, venturing out just a couple of times into the village, huddling under an umbrella as she circuited the tiny centre, looking in shop windows, familiarising herself with what had changed. A small nail salon had opened up, run by a girl from her class at school, and Willow River Farm, run by Martin Donbury, now had a farm shop just past the church. Lily went inside and bought a couple of bags of potatoes from a surprised Jimmy Donbury, who didn't recognise her until she told him her name. She had recognised him: his face was still as roundly cherubic as it had been at school, now with just a hint of stubble, although his shoulders had grown wide and his stomach even wider. For a few minutes they reminisced over their school days, before Lily bade him farewell.

Mary was pleased to see her again, and they shared a damp afternoon coffee, talking about old times. As Mary frequently moved the conversation onto her current children and imminent birth, Lily was reminded of how

98

different their lives were, even though, now that she was living back in the village, she was beginning to feel some of the old connections. Mary was surprised to find Lily was working at the guesthouse, and Lily learned that Mary's mother had indeed worked there for a few years, mostly helping out when they were busy.

'I was wondering,' Lily asked, having taken up the offer of another cup of coffee, 'Do you remember a writer called Victoria Borton who used to visit sometimes? She wrote a famous book—'

Mary shook her head while clicking her fingers at the same time. 'I most certainly do. She wrote *The Trainspotter's Guide to Romance*. I loved that book. I wore out my original copy, I read it so many times. And the movie … well, it wasn't quite as good, but I still probably watched it a dozen times. I mean, my Andy thought it sucked, but he would, he's a man. You have seen it, haven't you?'

Lily decided not to forfeit her cool—or dork, depending on Mary's point of view—points by admitting she'd only watched it a couple of days ago. She shrugged and said, 'Of course. Not really my thing, but it was all right.'

'I wonder what happened to her, eh?' Mary said. 'I mean, I went and read all of her books. None of the others were as good, but I figured she'd just hit her stride. She just kind of disappeared, though, didn't she?'

Lily nodded. 'Ah, yeah. Perhaps she made so much money she retired to the Caribbean.'

Mary leaned forward, an earnest look on her face. 'You know what I think? I reckon she's holed up somewhere, desperately trying to write a follow up, but she can't because that book was so good. And the trying is driving her mad.'

Lily considered asking Mary to predict Saturday's

National Lottery numbers, then thought better of it, just in case. Life was weird enough already.

'I'm going for the Caribbean island,' she said.

'I bet you'll find I'm right,' Mary said, chuckling. 'My Andy says I should work for the government. You know, I knew it was going to rain today.'

'How about tomorrow?' Lily asked.

Mary pouted and peered up at the ceiling, as though the weather forecast could be read in the swirling plasterboard patterns, then looked back at Lily and grinned. 'Sunny in the morning, cloudy in the afternoon,' she said.

'Umbrella?'

'Maybe take one just in case.'

'Got it.'

The next morning, it was absolutely chucking down, the rain bombarding the village in fat drops so heavy that Lily couldn't even ride the bike down to the annexe, but instead donned a pair of Wellington boots and huddled under the umbrella, the hamper wrapped in a plastic bag. Even so, by the time she reached the annexe, she was soaked from the waist down and any fantastical dreams that might have been building felt washed away, as she stood outside Victoria's door like a sodden cat waiting to be let in from the rain.

To her surprise, Victoria was wearing only a grey jogging tracksuit, but her bare feet defied any chance that she was going to make a couple of turns of the cycle path in the rain.

'Ah, Tiffany, thank goodness. Where have you been the last couple of days? I thought you'd left.'

'No, just a couple of days off. Every Wednesday and Thursday, although Gus said maybe Tuesdays too in November, as midweek trade tends to fall off a cliff once the leaves have fallen.'

'No. You absolutely must not. I need you. The last two days, I've barely been able to eat or sleep. Just a tuna sandwich or two, and well, enough coffee to wake the dead.'

'What happened?'

'Come in and I'll explain.'

Victoria took the hamper out of Lily's hands and beckoned her to follow with a jerk of her head. As Lily followed Victoria into the main bedroom suite, her eyes widened.

'You … tidied.'

Victoria set the hamper down on a table, then gave a sage nod of the head. 'Briefly,' she said, as though that explained everything. 'But I fear it could unravel at any moment, and the chaos….' She reached up both hands and rubbed at the sides of her head until her hair began to stick out with static. '…could return at any moment. I need the inspiration. Quickly, help me.'

'What do you need from me?'

'This girl, Lily. She lost everything and moved back in with her family. She meets a struggling writer when she starts working at a guesthouse … but what happens next?'

Lily stared at Victoria. The woman's hands had twisted into claws, like someone readying themselves to rip out a victim's heart. Her face had a look of anticipation that made Lily feel a little nervous.

'Ah … she, ah, she tries to help the woman … the writer, I mean. Because … she doesn't know what to do with her own life, so she figures she'll put the energy into helping someone else.'

Victoria, still staring at her, backed away until she bumped into her desk. Her hands scrabbled behind her until the fingers of one hand closed over a notepad. The other hand knocked over a jam jar filled with pens and pencils, but as they rattled against the tabletop Victoria didn't even turn around, just felt with her fingers until she found what she needed. Then, lifting the pad and pen, she nodded to Lily.

'Go on.'

'Ah … the writer has … issues. Yes, issues. She's a … ah, recluse. She's scared to go outside but the girl … helps her. They become friends—'

'A twist!' Victoria wailed with such sudden ferocity that Lily took a step back and nearly tripped over a stool near the door behind her. 'We need a preliminary twist to drag the reader in, one that sinks its claws into their soft, pliable minds and will not let go!'

'Okay … well … how about the writer … has a secret.'

Victoria's eyes widened. 'Yes. A secret. What's the secret?'

'You're a writer, you tell me.'

Victoria blinked. 'Yes. Yes, you're right. I will give it some thought.' She dropped the pad and pen back on the table and turned to the hamper, lifting the lid. 'You may wait downstairs, Tiffany. Oh … what on earth is this?'

'Potato salad,' Lily said with a shy smile. 'But I doubled up the bacon today so you don't feel too perturbed.'

'A thoughtful girl, you are,' Victoria said. 'Now leave me.'

Lily didn't want to be told again, hurrying downstairs to the lounge room where she hunted through a couple of drawers until she found a towel to dry herself with. Then, she waited until the call came from upstairs.

She found the hamper sitting outside the closed door.

The lid wasn't closed properly, and when Lily lifted it she caught sight of a piece of paper taped to the underside.

What's the secret?

She smiled before pocketing the piece of paper.

On the walk back to the guesthouse, she would give it some thought.

16

KICKING THE BEEHIVE

'SO ... SHE NEVER GOES OUTSIDE?'

Uncle Gus shrugged. 'Not that we know of.' Then, grinning, he gave a shake of his bushy hair and widened his eyes. 'Perhaps she goes outside in the dark and stalks around like some kind of vampire. Ooooh.'

Aunt Gert slapped him on the arm. 'Don't be ridiculous. She's busy writing another book. That's why she doesn't go outside. She gets food deliveries so she doesn't need to go shopping, and she has those crazy fans wandering around—'

'Nutters, the lot of them,' Uncle Gus said. 'Those orange anoraks are like warning lights for psychopaths.'

Lily laughed. 'I don't think they're that bad.'

'I expect they glow in the dark. They make pairs and run down the cycle path going "choo choo!"' Uncle Gus slapped his leg and chortled, making Lily fearful he was going to be sick.

'Look, don't make fun of them,' Aunt Gert said. 'Or her. It can't be easy being famous.'

'Especially when you go from being a bit famous to

really famous practically overnight,' Lily said. 'No wonder she doesn't go outside.'

Aunt Gert narrowed her eyes. 'I get the feeling you've got a pet project going on,' she said to Lily. 'Are you going to bring her back into the world?'

'I wouldn't go that far, but I might see if I can get her to go outside,' Lily said.

'Well, good luck with that,' Uncle Gus said. 'She's been in there for years and the only time I can remember her coming out was when we had a power cut one night and the phone line went down. And even then, it was only to complain about the lack of hot water.'

'And she waited until it was dark before she came,' Aunt Gert said. 'Gave me a terrible fright to find her knocking on the restaurant window. She was dressed all in black and even had a woolly hat pulled down to her eyes. I thought it was a serial killer.'

'I'll see if I can encourage her to wear brighter clothes,' Lily said.

The next morning, however, when she arrived at the annexe with Victoria's breakfast hamper, she found a note pinned to the outside of the door:

Creation in Progress
DO **NOT** *Disturb*
(Leave the hamper, knock once,
Then come back at <u>ten o'clock</u>)

Lily did as she was asked, putting the hamper down, knocking loudly once, then retreating to the end of the corridor, where she hid at the top of the stairs, peering around to see what happened.

After a few seconds, the door cracked open, and a walking cane poked out, its hooked end catching under the hamper's handle and dragging in inside. The door closed with a soft thump.

It was a much nicer day, so instead of waiting downstairs, Lily went outside and cycled along the cycle path for a couple of miles until she reached the first of three tunnels on the way to Exeter. The tunnel was beside a wider section of the river where Lily remembered going to swim with her friends in the summer, although in those days they'd had to ride along the main road because the old railway line was still a mess of brambles and hawthorn bushes. It was too cold to swim now in mid-September, but it was pleasant enough for a picnic and a little bird-watching or fishing. She remembered fondly the time a group of friends and her had decided to camp here one night, and she'd had hopes of maybe sharing a campfire kiss with her crush at the time, Mark Birt from the year above, only for Tim Johnson and Jimmy Donbury to start telling ghost stories and daring the girls to run through the tunnel in the dark. Mary had started crying, and in the end Lily had taken her to a phone box up on the main road where she had called Mary's parents to come and pick her up. By the time Lily had got back, Mark had got cozy with a girl from the Lower Sixth Form and that was the end of that.

She sat down on a bench overlooking the river and let her thoughts drift. She felt happy in a way she hadn't in some time, but a feeling of impermanence persisted, as though at some point soon she would have to up sticks again and move on. She had a degree, training, experience in the financial sector, connections. A life as a waitress and cleaner wasn't what she had set out for. But it was nice, peaceful, and sometimes, she wondered, maybe that was enough. Uncle Gus and Aunt Gert certainly seemed happy, whereas all she remembered from her years in London was the stress of getting from one meeting to another, making sure she was brushed up for every client, having to mull over every word. And that was before the traffic jams, and the sirens, and the guy spilling coffee on her in the street, and the builders, and the tube delays and the——

Lily slapped a hand down on the damp wood of the bench, feeling the soft cushion of lichen growing over parts of its surface, the cracks where rain had got through the varnish, the chips where bits were starting to flake off.

'Relax,' she said aloud. 'Take it easy.'

A couple of rainbow trout swam languidly through the water, the sun glinting off their backs. Lily thought about how peaceful it must be to be a fish, your only real task to sift through some silt in search of a bit of food for the day, then noticed a fisherman walking through the field on the other side of the river, a rod over his shoulder and a box of tackle in his hand, and figured that fish had their problems too.

Giving the fisherman a quick wave and a good morning, she headed off back to the annexe, secretly hoping he didn't catch anything.

The hamper was where she had been told to collect it, the note still on the door. Lily briefly considered knocking, then thought better of it. However, the hamper's lid wasn't closed straight, so Lily lifted the edge to readjust the wicker hooks at the sides, and saw another slip of paper inside.

What's the SECRET…?

The capitalisation and ellipsis suggested a sense of urgency. Lily looked at it for a moment, noticing a smudge on one corner that could have been ink, then put it in her pocket, picked up the hamper, and headed back to the guesthouse.

A couple of guests had just arrived that morning, so Lily helped her uncle and aunt get them organised, showing them the room, the common areas, explaining meal times, and answering a few questions that they had. After the new arrivals had headed out for the day, and Uncle Gus and Aunt Gert had settled down in the restaurant with a chess board between them, Lily hijacked the reception computer for a little research.

First, however, she couldn't resist checking the social media she had been staunchly avoiding.

As before, there was even less of note, and almost nothing of any great importance. It felt as though her abstinence from posting inane pictures or pointless status updates had set her adrift, and she was slowly being forgotten. She glanced over her shoulder, through a little window in the reception door which looked into the restaurant, and saw Uncle Gus, gripping a handful of his hair like a pauper's bunch of flowers, shaking his head while Aunt Gert chuckled.

The guesthouse had a website through which you could make reservations, as well as listings on most of the major booking websites, but otherwise her aunt and uncle had no social media presence at all. And they looked carefree, happy. The stress and trauma of the online world was something of which they were entirely unaware.

Wanting to switch off, but unable to resist, Lily brought

up Steve's profile. Since his last picture, there was only one new update: a brief status that simply said: OMG, I can't believe it, followed by a crying face emoji. A couple of dozen people had written comments to the tune of oh no, what's happened?, but Steve was yet to reply. Lily wondered if he'd been dumped by his new tramp, or whether something far less dramatic had happened—such as a loss of car keys, or a coffee spillage on one of the messes he called art—and he was hamming it up for the cameras. Lily thought about making a comment to that effect, then realised with a sudden sense of freedom, that she didn't care.

Instead, she went back to her primary intention, which was to research a little more on Victoria Borton. Part of her thought it might be fun to suggest a secret that had actually come from Victoria's own past. However, writers weren't the gossip factories that most TV celebrities and movie stars were, and there was nothing of any great interest besides a couple of short "What happened to …" blog posts and an article from two years ago claiming a follow up to *The Trainspotter's Guide to Romance* was in the works, simply titled *The Trainspotter's Guide to Messy Breakups*. However, noticing the date—April 1st—seemed to suggest that the comments underneath, claiming it was a hoax, were most likely correct.

It looked like rather than building a wave of expectation among fans a la Harper Lee or George RR Martin—a few stalker-types aside—Victoria was swiftly being forgotten by the wider reading community. Eight years was a long time even for a writer.

After a brief search for "cool secrets for writers", which uncovered such gems as "the main character has a box under his/her bed which contains the heart of his missing ex-lover, wrapped in a pink ribbon", and "when he/she shows up at the ranch they bought online, they find it comes with a zoo … and the locks on the cages are wearing thin!", she figured she might as well have a quick search for Victoria's son before she decided to pull the plug on her social media forever.

Unsurprisingly, Michael Borton was a pretty common name, returning almost fifty search results. Initially overawed and on the verge of giving up, however, closer inspection of profile pictures allowed her to narrow it down to less than a dozen who either fit by rough age, or had nothing visible to rule them out.

Briefly she typed a note:

Hello! You don't know me—or you've almost certainly forgotten me, because it's possible we did in fact meet as children—my name is Lily Markham, and I work at Willow River Guesthouse in Willow River, Devon. I'm trying to find the son of the writer, Victoria Borton. If you're him, please reply. Thanks! Lily.

It was worth a shot. Lily shrugged as she looked at the list of messages in her sent box, then switched off the computer.

In the restaurant, Uncle Gus was now standing up, both hands holding clumps of his hair as though attempting to become his own puppet master.

'Just knock your king over,' Aunt Gert said. 'It's checkmate in two. You can't get out of it.'

'There's always a way out,' Uncle Gus said, shaking his head.

'No, there really isn't.' Aunt Gert leaned forward. 'You have two possible moves, here or here.' She pointed at the board. 'Both mean I can go here, and then you lose.' She clapped her hands together and rocked back on the chair, wincing as the plaster cast over her knee hit the underside of the table. 'Tell him, Lily.'

'I can't play chess.'

Aunt Gert nodded at the window. 'It looks like rain again, so now's a good time to learn.'

With a grunt of frustration, Uncle Gus reached down and knocked over his king. 'All right, you've got me. I'm going to go and cut some cabbages. Beat her for me, Lily.'

Lily smiled as Uncle Gus stomped off. Aunt Gert, chuckling, replaced the pieces. 'Right, it's pretty easy. First you have to move this one,' she said.

'Aunt Gert,' Lily said, 'do you know any good secrets?'

'About what?'

'About anything. Like, a kind of plot twist for a movie.' She waved her arms in the air. 'Woah, he's not a clown, he's a secret agent, that kind of thing.'

'Careful, dear, you'll knock over the pieces.'

'Sorry.'

'Hmm.' Aunt Gert frowned. 'A secret can be anything, big or small. It depends on what you're trying to do, doesn't it?'

'Surprise people.'

'Then you make it as outrageous as possible.'

'But … I literally have no idea. I've spent my whole life moving big numbers around. It's maths. I know maths, because it's logical, and predictable. I'm not good with the unpredictable.'

Aunt Gert grinned. 'Perhaps you should try going on a blind date.'

'Absolutely no chance. I'm still in mourning over Steve.'

'Are you really? Because it doesn't seem like it. You seem to be coping very well. If I were to hazard a guess, it would be that Steve had become part of your routine, and that only by shaking up the bag a little bit did you figure out that he wasn't really needed.'

'Shaking up the bag.…'

'Sometimes we have to step out of our comfort zone. You can step back into it, of course, but if you don't roll those dice once in a while, you could be missing out on things that might change your life.'

'Have you ever tried stepping out of your comfort zone?'

'Absolutely. When I agreed to go on a date with that great bear in there. I didn't find him attractive at all. I thought—and don't tell him this—he was a monster. I'd never seen a man so unattractive.' She giggled. 'So I made him grow that beard.'

'Really?'

Aunt Gert slapped a hand on the table so hard the chess pieces jumped. 'Ha, not at all. But I really didn't like him. And then, after I went out with him … I found out that I did. And the rest is history. I'm fully in my comfort zone now, but I wouldn't have been without stepping outside it.'

'How would I step outside my comfort zone?'

'All sorts of ways. You're doing it right now by working here. And have you thought about going on a date with someone?'

'Not at all. I'd be on the rebound.'

'What's the craziest kind of person you could go on a date with? What kind of job would they have?'

'Ah … a poet?'

Aunt Gert rolled her eyes. 'Be realistic, dear. That's not a job.'

'Well … how about a farmer. I wouldn't go out with one in a million years.'

'There you go. Find a young farmer and go out with them. What about Jimmy Donbury up in the farm shop? He's a nice lad.'

'No! I used to get on at the same bus stop.'

Aunt Gert grinned. 'Go on, ask him out for a drink. You might find you like him.'

'I thought we were talking about secrets?'

Aunt Gert grinned. 'Throw a rock into the cave a couple of times and see what comes out.'

17

NIGHT OUT

STILL QUITE UNSURE HOW ASKING AUNT GERT TO suggest an interesting secret had turned into being coerced into asking Jimmy Donbury out for a drink, Lily duly made her attempt to kick the beehive after she finished work at three o'clock, heading up to the farm shop where she found Jimmy weighing potatoes and sealing them into bags.

'Alright?'

'Hey, Jimmy.'

'What're you after, Lily?'

'Ah....' Her skin began to tingle. 'I was just wondering what you were up to this evening. Fancy a pint in The Crown?'

There, it was said. Far easier than she had expected, the words had moved slowly off her tongue in a wedding—or perhaps funeral—procession.

'Be nice to catch up, eh,' Jimmy said, showing none of the nerves that would suggest he understood the severity of her request. 'Been a while, hasn't it?'

'Seven?'

'Got to bring some heifers in then, so what about eight?'

'Sure.'

'You want a bag of spuds? Two for one.'

'Uh … why not?'

On the way home, lugging two five-kilogram bags of potatoes she hoped her mum would have a use for, Lily stopped in to see Mary—hoping to get a prediction for tonight's date—but Mary had gone off to pick her kids up from school, and the person on duty in the café was an old woman Lily didn't recognise. She ordered a coffee and sat for a while, thinking things over, then gave the surprised old woman a bag of potatoes on the way out before heading for home. It was only five o'clock, but she needed to decide which pair of Wellington boots would be best for her date.

Her dad was in the garage, working on a sun mural made out of plastic bottle tops, a glue gun in one hand, a large plastic container slung around his neck, filled to the brim with bottle tops of all colours.

'Where'd you get those?' Lily asked.

Pete grinned. 'The supermarket recycle bins,' he said. 'They were only too pleased to offload them. Said I could have as many as I want.'

The sun reminded her of one of those weird dream sequences in *Watership Down* when the sun god talked to Hazel, and she had to admit, her dad was quite the artist. She wasn't sure how long she'd been staring into the blend of colours when Pete nudged her arm.

'Ah, love, your eyes'll go funny. Nice to know it'll have an impact. It's for the sustainable development exposition at Brentwell Art Gallery. Off out tonight? You look nice. I'd change out of those boots, though.'

Lily gave her head a little shake, then turned to her dad.

'I'm going on a date with Jimmy Donbury,' she said.

'Well … nice lad,' Pete said. 'He ask you out?'

'Ah … I asked him.'

Pete lifted an eyebrow. 'Not sure that you're going to get your own back on a London artist by dating a Devonshire farmer. But if you really like him—'

Lily frowned. 'Aunt Gert suggested it. She wants me to break out of my comfort zone.'

Pete chuckled. 'Did she get onto the "Angus is a monster but I still love him" topic again? She brings that one out practically every time I see her. I don't think she can quite believe it herself.'

'Something like that.'

'Well, have a nice time. Don't go disrespecting the lad. He's down-to-earth, but he's a nice lad. We always share a chat up at the farmer's market and occasionally he'll stop in at the park for a hotdog.'

'I won't.'

'That's my girl.'

Sarah had gone out—to a Village Council meeting, no less—so Lily idled around the house for a bit, changing clothes three times, before finally heading out to The Crown just before eight. She arrived five minutes fashionably late, and pushed through the doors to find a group of young men crowded around the bar.

'And then, I said to him … your trotters have gone south!'

The group exploded with laughter, several guys slapping the bar, one nearly falling off his stool. Lily approached cautiously, finding Jimmy Donbury at the group's centre, a pint half drunk in front of him.

'Lily, there you are. Lads, do you remember Lily Markham? Hotdog Pete's lass.'

Lily grinned. 'Hotdog Pete on the sharpshooter,' she said, making gun fingers with her right hand and firing off a couple of pretend bullets.

There was a scattering of muted laughter. Lily gave a grim smile.

'Sandpit Lils,' one guy muttered, and it took her a long hard stare to look back through twenty years of aging and maturity to recognise Colin Beecham, two years below her at school, and who had been famous back in primary school for eating his own socks.

'Hey, Colin,' she said.

'Ha, you remember me. Working up at Wright's, lawnmower section. Where are you these days?'

'Frying eggs and making beds at Willow River Guesthouse,' Lily said.

'She's a poet and she don't notice it!' Jimmy chortled, banging a hand on the bar, missing the rhyme of the phrase, as the other guys around them laughed.

'Didn't you get some posh job in the smoke?' came a reedy, girly voice from a short, dumpy guy she couldn't quite remember. That was it … Womble. So called because he allegedly only had one ball, after a monkey bars accident in the First Year. Wow, the years had been harsh, making him even shorter and dumpier than ever. Or maybe she had grown, she wasn't sure.

'William Jones? Is that you?'

'She called him William,' someone else chortled, and a sudden rattle of stools announced the group getting to their feet, clapping their hands together. 'Womble … Womble … the Womble of Willow River is he!'

The whole pub seemed to shake with the raucous song, but as quick as it had begun, it went silent, the group stepping aside, leaving William standing alone in the centre.

'The Womble of Willow River is me!' he wailed in his high-pitched voice, doing an awkward dance step, his elbows bumping up and down, followed by another hail of wild laughter.

'Whose round is it?' Jimmy said, clapping his hands together, as the others patted Womble on the back and sipped their pints.

'Mine!' Lily shouted, putting up a hand. 'What are you all having?'

'Pint.'

'Pint.'

'Pint.'

'Pint.'

'Pint.'

'Pint … hey, Lils,' Jimmy said, 'Why don't you get us some of those posh London drinks you see on the telly?'

Lily smiled. 'All right, why not?' She racked her brains, trying to remember the kind of cocktails her friends had often ordered, usually while Lily sat quietly drinking a half of lager.

'I'll have six Apple and Rhubarb Tatankas,' she said, leaning through the group and beckoning the barman over. 'Large.'

The barman nodded. 'Ah … what's in that then?'

It was a little after eleven when she got home, her head buzzing, and a wide grin on her face. She had lost three games of triples pool, but somehow managed to win the darts, despite not having played since university, then held her own when the group moved into the skittles hall at the pub's rear, winning one game but coming spectacularly last in another.

Pete was watching the end of a James Bond film when Lily came into the living room and slumped down into an armchair.

'Hey, Hotdog,' she slurred.

'You had a good time, then? How was the date?'

'I don't think Jimmy realised we were supposed to be going out, just the two of us.'

'Are you disappointed?'

'Not at all. It was awesome. I haven't seen most of those guys in years. I signed up for the skittles team, and next Sunday afternoon I've going fishing up at the reservoir with Rod and Womble.'

'You're going fishing with someone called Rod?'

Lily broke down into uncontrollable sniggering. She hadn't even noticed at the time. 'Rod … yeah, he works in the tackle shop in Brentwell. Rod … oh my.'

'Womble, he's a nice lad. See him when he collects the bins on a Tuesday. He's got two kids. One of them comes to the art class I run on Monday afternoons. Only five, but he's a creative little guy. Made a stegosaurus out of egg boxes last week.'

'I didn't realise I was crashing boys' Wednesday. Jimmy didn't mention it, but said it was nice to have a token girl around.'

'No one caught your eye, then?'

Lily sighed. 'Dad … am I a snob? I mean, they were all really nice, and we had a great time, but it's just … none of them … I don't know … I'm too choosey, aren't I?'

Pete shifted uncomfortably. 'You'd probably be better off discussing this with your mother.'

'The Second-to-Worst Witch?' Lily sniggered again, remembering the nickname given to her mother by Colin, whose younger sister apparently worked in the little electronics shop next door to Sarah's craft shop.

Pete smiled. 'Don't let her hear you say that. She hates it. But you can call me Hotdog all day long.'

'I'm a snob, I know I am.'

'You're a little drunk, but that's all. There's no harm in being picky, and you did just come out of a relationship.'

'Not by intent,' Lily said, then immediately felt a little weepy. She stood up, swayed a little, then announced she was going to bed, keen to get out of her dad's presence before she started to cry.

In her bedroom, she changed into her pyjamas and lay down. After a few minutes of sleeplessness, she got up, opened a drawer and pulled out the laptop she had brought with her from London, intending to stalk Steve, maybe to send him a message, maybe just to write something cynical on one of his more recent status updates … but to her surprise she had five new messages, all of them from Michael Borton.

Four were false alarms, but the fifth was far more interesting.

Lily—firstly, thanks for your message! This is Michael Borton, and yes, my mother is a writer. You found her—thank you! Could you please tell me where she is? For the last five years I've felt like she dropped off the face of the Earth.

18

MOVING OUTSIDE

THE THUMPING HANGOVER THAT GREETED LILY THE next morning at first was enough to make her forget about the mysterious message. Then, as she sat eating breakfast with her dad—her mum having long before headed out to the shop—she opened up her laptop for a casual browse and remembered.

Michael Borton … Victoria's son. She had found the little boy in the photograph. But what to do now?

'Any job offers?' Pete asked.

Lily smiled. 'None yet.'

'Well, you'd better get a move on or you'll be late,' Pete said, finishing his cornflakes and standing up.

'I'm just on my way,' Lily said, peering at the screen.

'Has Steve got in touch again?'

Lily shook her head. 'No, someone far more interesting.'

Pete chuckled. 'Well, good luck with it. Hotdog Pete is out of here.' Lily cringed, but Pete laughed again. 'See you later, sweetheart. Have a good day.'

It took a couple of paracetamol to improve things, but Lily was feeling a lot better by the time she got to the guesthouse, just in time to start making breakfast for the guests. Luckily, the large group had departed, and only a pair of couples remained. Even so, the smell of the eggs and bacon made Lily feel a little queasy. By the time she headed out with Victoria's breakfast, she couldn't bear to be inside.

The bike ride didn't help, but it was a fine day with a few wisps of cloud in the sky. Lily parked her bike outside the annexe, but just as she was about to go inside, she had an idea.

How long had it been since Victoria had been outside?

Thinking quickly, Lily went around to the annexe's rear, to the patch of grass crying out to be turned into a picnic area and playground. The picnic tables around the front were too heavy to move on her own, so she went inside, rooting around on the bottom floor until she found a store cupboard with a fold-out table and a couple of deckchairs inside. Then, taking them around the back, she set them up on the grass underneath Victoria's window.

Setting the hamper down, she went upstairs. The DO NOT DISTURB sign had gone. Lily gave a light knock, and a moment later the door swung open.

Victoria looked almost normal in jeans and a thick grey roll-neck sweater. Only the pink sunglasses propped up in her hair were out of place.

'Ah, good morning,' Lily said.

'Penelope, there you are. You're five minutes late, but we won't worry about that.'

'I'm afraid I've pulled a muscle in my shoulder,' Lily said, not bothering to correct Victoria, but instead giving her shoulder a dramatic rub and wincing to add effect. 'I couldn't bring the hamper up the stairs this morning, but it's a lovely day, so I've set you up a table outside.'

Victoria's face dropped. She stared at Lily as though she'd just been told her dog had died.

'What?'

'It's … ah … outside.'

'Outside?'

'Yes. Outside.'

'I can't go outside.' Victoria frowned. 'I don't … know the way.'

Her voice had taken on such a childlike fragility that Lily suddenly felt sorry for her. By all accounts the millions she had made from her books and the movie version of *A Trainspotter's Guide to Romance* couldn't help her with one simple thing: overcoming her social anxiety.

Lily put out a hand. 'I can help you,' she said. 'Don't worry, there's no one around.'

Victoria frowned again. For a moment Lily thought she was going to step back inside and slam the door. Then, she reached out a tentative hand and put it on Lily's shoulder.

'I haven't been outside in … years,' she said.

'It hasn't changed much,' Lily said. 'Well, the grass is a bit longer. I keep telling Uncle Gus to come up and cut it.'

'Well, not to worry. Perhaps he could consider getting a goat or something.'

'I'll mention it when I go back.'

Victoria was still leaning on Lily's shoulder, looking uncomfortable. 'Am I hurting you, dear? You said you'd pulled a muscle.'

'Ah … other shoulder.'

'Right.'

'You're going to need shoes.'

'Oh. Of course.'

Victoria reached a foot behind the half-open door and pushed a pair of slip-on shoes into view. The accumulation of dust on their upper surface broke Lily's heart. She watched as Victoria slid them on, dust bunnies falling away.

'Oh, they barely fit anymore.'

'It's only a short way.'

'Right.'

'Are you ready?'

Victoria took a deep breath and gave a slow nod. 'Yes.'

Lily stepped backwards. Victoria, still leaning on her, had no choice but to step forward into the corridor. Pausing after each step at first, Lily helped her along the corridor to the stairs, where Victoria paused again, her breath coming faster.

'I'm not sure I can do it,' she said. 'It's so dark.'

'That's only because the light bulb's blown,' Lily said. 'Something else I'll mention to Uncle Gus when I get back.'

She went first, holding on to Victoria's arm, leading her slowly down. She felt like a nurse in a care home, bringing an elderly patient down to meet their family, even though Victoria's ailments were purely psychological. Even so, as Victoria's movements began to get smoother—even briefly letting go of Lily to take hold of the narrow staircase's banister—Lily sensed Victoria's reclusiveness was more a reluctance to go outside and case of habit rather than any genuine psychological disorder. Once they were down the stairs and into the common area, Victoria began to take more interest in her surroundings than in where she put her feet.

'Oh, is that how it used to look? I remember that little train. I used to take Michael up to Exeter to look around the shops. The view was quite delightful....'

As they reached the back door, Lily let out a little gasp. Immediately Victoria tensed, but Lily grabbed hold of her arm before she could think to flee.

'I'm so sorry,' she said, staring at the table outside, the hamper sat on top. 'That little sod….'

A squirrel was fussing around on top of the hamper, making occasional attempts to find a way inside. Lily stared as it nibbled at the wicker, then tried to lift the lid, getting one paw inside before it slipped shut again.

'I'll shoo it off,' she said, starting to move forward, but it was Victoria this time who grabbed her arm.

'No, don't. He's so … pretty.'

They watched for a couple of minutes as the little squirrel continued his explorations. Then, suddenly figuring it out, he pushed his nose into the gap between the lid and the basket, and disappeared inside.

'Okay, now you can stop him,' Victoria said, squeezing Lily's shoulder.

Lily darted forward, flapping her hands at the squirrel, which reappeared from the hamper and scampered down off the table, running to the safety of a nearby tree. Lily lifted the lid, and to her relief, found the cling film covering the food remained intact. She looked up to beckon Victoria outside, but at the sight of the empty doorway, her heart dropped.

Victoria was gone.

Lily dropped the hamper lid, gave the tree with its hiding squirrel a warning glare, then dashed back to the annexe's rear door and went inside.

'Victoria? Victoria!'

'Oh, Penelope, I'm right here.'

Lily jumped. Rather than retreating back upstairs as Lily had expected, Victoria had moved closer to the wall and was standing on tiptoes as she looked at a large framed photograph of the station building in the nineteen sixties.

'It's changed so much, hasn't it?' Victoria said. 'I mean … look at all those people. And the thrill of the train coming into the station … you know, that's what I always loved about train stations. That sense of adventure, of motion. And all those people, every one of them a character study. It's not the same now, is it?'

Lily smiled. 'But when you think about it, the best bits are still here. The platform and the station building, even the line where the tracks went. And the view, the nature.'

'You're a very pure girl, aren't you?'

Lily wrinkled her nose. She considered herself a lot of things, but the idea of being pure had never crossed her mind.

'Do you think so?'

'Yes. And pure girls are wonderful, don't you think? A blank canvas, waiting for the world to write down their story. What's the secret, dear? Do you know?'

Lily frowned, thinking about the message from Michael. She hadn't yet replied, but planned to do so after she had cleared up the breakfast things.

'The writer in the story … she's estranged from her son. I haven't decided quite how yet. But the girl … she decides to help the writer out by reuniting them. Only, there's a twist….'

'That's a nice idea, but what's the twist, dear?'

Lily smiled. 'The son, when he arrives, he's really good-looking, and the girl … she falls in love with him.'

'That's a little melodramatic, don't you think?'

Lily shrugged. 'I'd read it.'

'And you're not much of a reader … hmm … we could be on to something. Well, that's nice, but it's not really a secret. It's a conflicting device. We need a secret, some big reveal.'

Lily shook her head. 'I don't know. You're the writer, you tell me.'

Victoria sighed. 'That's the problem, isn't it? I can't get my brain to work like it used to. It's plagued me for years. I don't know what to do.'

'Well, I certainly know what you could do next.'

'What's that?'

'Come outside and eat your breakfast before that pesky squirrel comes back.'

19

MIXED MESSAGES

It had taken another few minutes of goading to finally get Victoria out to the table, by which time any lingering heat in the baked beans was long gone. Once outside, however, Victoria seemed to relax, and although Lily went for a walk along the river while she ate, Victoria was still there when Lily came back, leaning back on one chair with her feet up on the seat of the other, gazing out across the overgrown meadow towards the V-shaped forest in the valley between the two nearest hills.

'Weather permitting, I'd like to take breakfast outside again tomorrow,' she said, as Lily collected the hamper and secured it to the back of the bicycle. 'And if it rains, perhaps inside the common area there?'

Lily nodded. 'With pleasure,' she said.

An hour later, after tidying up the breakfast things and dealing with any tasks Uncle Gus and Aunt Gert had for her, she made for the computer on the reception desk and loaded up her messages. She hadn't imagined the message from Michael. It was still there, so she started typing a reply. Halfway in, though, she lost her nerve, deleted it, and started all over again.

After three more aborted attempts, the best she could do was: *Hi Michael, this is Lily. Thanks for getting in touch. Your mother is staying at the guesthouse where I work, trying, I believe, to write a book. She doesn't go out much. Is everything all right between you two?*

She sent it before she could stop herself, then immediately scrabbled around, looking for some button to unsend it. Too late, the message was marked as received. Lily scowled. She sounded like a social worker. She waited a couple of minutes for a reply, but none came. Of course, he probably had a normal job where he couldn't just play on social media all morning. Or perhaps he thought she was an idiot.

Or both.

The bell jingled as someone came in from outside, and Lily snapped back to attention. She reached up, adjusting the name tag pinned to her chest that Uncle Gus had given her—and that Victoria had dutifully ignored on multiple occasions—and adopted her best welcoming smile.

'Good morning. Welcome to Willow River Guesthouse. Are you looking for a room?'

The woman looked up and grinned nervously. A little overweight, short, and with greasy hair pressed under a beanie hat with a tractor logo on the front, her teeth were spaced out too much for her to be attractive, and she had a pimple on her chin that really needed either squeezing or concealing. And the beige that permeated her clothing needed replacing.

'I'm looking for someone,' she said.

'Not a room?'

The woman put a book on the counter and turned it over to reveal Victoria's author picture.

'This lady. I heard she lived around here. I just wondered if you knew her—'

Lily shook her head. 'I'm afraid not. She … have you asked in the farmer's market? They get a lot more business than we do. If she does live round here, they'd surely know.'

The woman's eyes brightened. 'Oh? Really? I'll go and ask. Thank you very much.'

She shuffled out before Lily could say anything, leaving Lily staring at the closing door, wondering whether she'd been too harsh, unkind, or not harsh enough. She had thought of sending her on to where Jimmy Donbury worked as a kind of joke, but perhaps she could talk to Victoria about actually engaging with some of these people. After all, if she had genuine fans, shouldn't she be flattered? Or had something happened with one of these stalker types that had forced her into being a recluse in the first place?

She had left her message page open on the sent message to Michael, and before she could stop herself, she added a little postscript: *She still seems popular, judging by the people that sometimes come by, looking for her. Did something happen?*

She sent the message, then reread it and wished she hadn't. In her original message, she hadn't even mentioned that Victoria had issues. Now, with the tone of her second message, she had suggested it.

A new message popped up in her inbox. From Michael. Lily stared, terrified to open it, but unable to resist.

Hi Lily,
Thanks for letting me know. Yeah, she had a bit of a meltdown after TTGTR blew up. Couldn't handle the attention. We had to have her

sectioned for a couple of months, but when she got out she did a disappearing act. I've been in touch with her publisher and agent, but even they don't know where she is. Please tell her I'm thinking about her, and I've love to see her again. I really appreciate you getting in contact with me. Thank you for putting my mind at rest.
Yours, Michael.

Lily stared. She started to type a reply, but thought better of it. She needed to take stock of everything and calm down before she did. Michael sounded so nice, so mature. She remembered the boy in the picture, looking at her, and wondered what kind of adult he had become. Was he handsome? Was he—

(we)

—married?

'Lily, screw it back on,' she muttered to herself, then gave the side of her head a tap. 'Numbers, numbers, numbers.'

Growing up with two artistic—and therefore often poor—parents, she had chosen to study maths, economics, and financial management for a reason. Numbers were logical. You could trust numbers. The emotive world—the art world, both inside the mind and out—were unpredictable. She had fallen completely for Steve, an artist, only to have her heart shattered. It surely wouldn't have happened if she'd fallen for a lawyer or a bank manager. Sure, they might have been a little boring, but they would certainly have been dependable.

Now, she felt an unhealthy compulsion to reply to Michael's message, in the vain hope that the young boy who had shown her such interest at the guesthouse's fiftieth anniversary would have grown into a modern day Prince Charming.

Not likely, but the idea was exciting.

She switched off the computer and stood up, forcing herself to walk away. There were bins that needed emptying, perhaps some pans had to be scraped, or she could go outside and pick dead leaves off the rose bushes. It was autumn, and winter would soon follow. Dark was approaching, dark and cold. Rain, long, windy nights, morning frost, and more rain. There was no reason to have any optimism.

However, when she looked out of the restaurant window, the sky was a clear, aquamarine blue, and the Willow River valley was as delightful and pristine as a travel agent's calendar.

Why couldn't she be optimistic? Why couldn't she dream?

Uncle Gus and Aunt Gert were getting out a Monopoly set—Devon Edition—and called to her to join them for a game. She hadn't played in years, but she had to satisfy her compulsion first.

'I'll be there in a sec,' she said.

'Which piece do you want? I'm the top hat, and Gert's the old boot.'

'I am not. I'm the car, as always.'

'I'll be the dog,' Lily said.

'Ah, you can't be the dog. We lost it a year or two back when we had a guesthouse tournament. You can be the plastic elephant we replaced it with.'

'What colour is it?'

'Pink.'

Lily smiled. 'Appropriate. I'll be right there. I just have one last thing to do.'

She hurried back to the computer and opened her messages before she could chicken out. Michael's message stood there like a shining beacon, waiting to be opened and reread. Lily typed a quick reply:

Dear Michael,

Thanks so much for getting in touch. I don't know the details of what happened to Victoria, but I think she might benefit if you could come up to see her. I can give you the guesthouse's address. You might even remember it. You stayed here when you were a child. I found a picture of you.
Yours,
Lily

She pressed send, then immediately felt her face flush, heat throbbing under her eyes. Her heart thundered, which was ridiculous, because it was only a message to a total stranger, and she hadn't exactly given him a come on. She took a deep breath, trying to calm her nerves. She could never beat Uncle Gus and Aunt Gert at Monopoly if she was so distracted.

Her inbox flashed with a new message. For a moment the whole world went grey with the thrill of it, then she crashed like a popped hot air balloon as she recognised the name attached.

Not Michael.

Steve.

Reluctantly, she opened it.

Hey Lils, saw you were online. Welcome back! Listen, so sorry. Can we talk? It's more than that, though. I'm in a bit of trouble, and I really need someone to get my back. I found an old postcard with your parents address. Is it okay if I pop down for a couple of days? I know you're upset but you might feel better when we're face to face.
Talk later,
Steve xxx

Lily stared at the message, whatever excitement she had felt now doused like a sodden British barbeque.

Could things possibly get worse?

'Lily, do you want us to start?'

Lily closed down her messages and went back into the restaurant, trying to put it all out of her mind. Steve wouldn't show up, would he? Michael wouldn't show up, either, surely? Or maybe they both would, and then they'd get in a big fight in the guesthouse car park. Or maybe Michael would turn out to be a weakling bank manager and Steve would hit him over the head with a paintbrush. Or perhaps they'd end up best friends, moving into the annexe downstairs from Victoria, and Lily would spend the rest of her life serving them breakfast while they built an increasingly elaborate system of model railways.

'Are you alright?' Aunt Gert said.

Lily realised she was standing in front of the table where her aunt and uncle sat, staring over their heads out into the guesthouse garden.

'I think I'm losing my mind,' she said.

'Ah, don't worry about that,' Aunt Gert said. 'It's probably just a bit of seasonal affective disorder. Sit down and relax. The coffee's brewing.'

'Bad news,' Uncle Gus said, as Aunt Gert scowled at him and gave a resigned shake of the head. 'You can't be the elephant because one of its legs broke off and now it won't stand up.'

'Angus sat on it,' Aunt Gert said.

For some reason, Lily found herself smiling, then giggling, and soon she was laughing so much she thought she might fall off the chair.

'I think you really have lost your mind,' Aunt Gert said. 'Now then. Shall we get started?'

20

MATCHMAKING

LILY STARED AT THE LINE OF MOWERS AND SHOOK HER head. 'I need something that's more powerful than a regular lawn mower, but not quite industrial,' she said, glancing at Colin Beecham, now dressed neatly in his Wright's Gardens uniform, and a baseball cap with HERE TO HELP across the front.

'You're aiming for proper lawn length?'

'Ah, yeah. Like, short. Uncle Gus has a Flymo he uses for the guesthouse garden, but I want to tackle that area by the old station. Uncle Gus said I could do what I want as long as I pay for it myself.'

Colin rubbed his chin and gave a sage nod.

'Well, I know the spot you mean.' He walked up to what looked like a miniature tractor with large protrusions at one end. Lily almost giggled; it looked like a red-faced man with a moustache.

'You want one of these babies first up,' Colin said. 'This'll take it right down to the turf. If you hit it regularly, though, you'll only need to use it twice a year.'

'How much is it?'

135

'Just under four grand.'

Lily nodded, wrinkling her nose. It was pricey, but it might be worth it. 'Do you take credit cards?'

'Good god, how much is Angus paying you?'

Lily shrugged. 'Savings.'

'Well, as you'll only need one a couple of times a year, I'd just go with a rental. Hundred and ten quid a day. After that you'll be good with one of those push petrol jobs. We've got one with a scratch on the casing that's half price. I'll drop off another ten percent if you buy me a pint in The Crown tonight.'

Lily grinned. 'It's a deal.'

Colin leaned closer. 'I heard Jimmy's picked up a bird, and he's bringing her out tonight to meet all the lads.'

Lily chuckled, wondering what exactly she had done to become "one of the lads". It was probably winning the darts, but it could also have been downing a pint of Worthington after a skittles team victory last Friday night, or landing a fourteen-pound trout last Sunday while Rod and Womble looked on with a mixture of amazement and awe. That she'd also known how to gut it and cook it over a hastily prepared barbeque had sealed her place in local folklore.

It was amazing what you could learn from YouTube.

'I wouldn't miss it for the world,' Lily said.

Lily wondered what Victoria would think when she turned up in a couple of days to cut the meadow behind the old station. Over the last week, she had managed to coax Victoria outside on two further occasions, but rain had curtailed the others and this morning the DO NOT

DISTURB sign had been up, and the hamper left outside with another note: *I'm still waiting for the secret.*

Lily wasn't sure what more she could say. She had given Victoria a variety of ideas, but Victoria had frowned and shook her head at some, flapped her hand dismissively at others.

'That's not a secret. That's a twist.'

'Well, that's not very likely, is it?'

'I'm writing a romance, not a horror story.'

'Would you really read a book where that happened?'

'You cannot kill off the main character!'

October had arrived quietly, September signing off with three days of rain before giving way to cooler mornings but brighter skies. Everything was becoming brown and orange, the leaves starting to change colour and some even to fall, scattering across the cycle path with every gust of wind. Lily swapped light sweaters for thicker roll-necks, a beanie hat her mum had knitted her, and a pretty scarf she had bought in a craft shop in Brentwell. Around the house, Sarah had been quiet, spending the lengthening evenings preparing Christmas-themed crafts for her shop, while Pete had been unable to keep the grin off his face after landing a contract to design a mural for an area of paving in Brentwell's Sycamore Park which had been assigned for restoration.

'I'm thinking of writing a book,' Lily announced, two glasses of wine into a celebratory dinner at Trevellian Head, a slightly posh restaurant halfway between Brentwell and Willow River. 'I mean, it can't be that hard, can it? What?'

A look had passed between her parents, Pete's lip curling into a half smile as Sarah responded with a raised eyebrow.

'I told you,' Pete said, grinning at Sarah. 'You can't be

born from as much collective creativity as us and spend your whole life dealing with numbers.'

'I was thinking of writing a maths textbook,' Lily said, hiccupping in the middle of "textbook", then glaring at her beef stroganoff as though it were to blame.

'Well, you go for it, dear,' Sarah said. 'Put a few pictures in to make it a bit more interesting. The ones we had at school were so dull that kids were dying in the middle of classes. Dropping like flies.'

Lily smiled. 'Maybe you could draw the front cover for me.'

'Are you really thinking of writing a maths textbook?' Pete asked.

Lily chuckled. 'No. Maybe some kind of story. Being back here … I kind of feel like it. In London, I never had time, nor the energy. And I never felt creative enough.'

'You were engaged to an artist,' Sarah said. Then, catching a look from Pete, she shrugged. 'Although perhaps that wasn't for the best.'

'I spent half my time listening to his issues and the other half worrying about them,' she said. 'And look where it got me. Oh, and by the way, he's threatening to visit me. He said he's in trouble.'

Sarah shrugged. 'Well, perhaps you could see what he has to say. He might have dealt with his issues.'

'He's not welcome in our house,' Pete said, stabbing a roast potato with a little too much intent. 'No one hurts my little girl and gets to walk straight back into her life.'

Lily gave Pete a pat on the arm. 'Thanks, Dad.'

'He'll never find it anyway,' Pete said. 'I have enough trouble myself on that road from Brentwell and I drive it every day.'

'He'll have GPS,' Lily said. 'Isn't there some way we

could hide the house? Like, hang a camouflage net over the gate or something?'

'I'll put up a charm to ward him off,' Sarah said.

'Thanks, Mum,' Lily said with a sigh. 'Can you put up another one to attract a new boyfriend?'

'No luck in the pub?'

Lily laughed. 'Great guys, but not my types.'

'I thought you were courting young Jimmy Donbury?' Sarah said, making both Pete and Lily cringe.

'I went for a pint with him and his mates,' Lily said. 'I don't think he even realised it was a date. And anyway, he's got a new girlfriend now.'

'Has he really?'

'A girl called Martina. One of Victoria Borton's fans. She showed up at the guesthouse looking for Victoria, and I sent her off to the farmer's market just to get rid of her. It turns out she's a trainee farm vet and is transferring down to Brentwell to be closer to Jimmy. You honestly can't make these things up.'

Sarah clapped her hands together. 'Well, good luck to them. And you should give yourself a pat on the back for bringing a little happiness into their lives.'

Lily theatrically reached around behind herself, then grimaced. 'I would, but I think I'd pull a muscle.'

'Ah, you need some Doreen,' Sarah said. 'I got the latest DVD through the post yesterday. 'Arm and body workout special. We'll have a go when we get home.'

Lily glanced at Pete, who hid a smile behind a roast potato. 'Can't wait.'

21

DRAWING OUT

Dear Lily,

Thanks for keeping me updated on my mother. It sounds like you've become friends with her, so I can only thank you again. I wonder if she ever mentions me? I would like to visit, but I'm worried I'll be a trigger for her problems. After all, it's been nearly five years without any contact. She's my mother, but she's also a unique person, as you've probably figured out. She was never easy to live with. However, if the bridge can be mended, I would like to mend it.
Kind regards,
Michael

LILY FELT A LITTLE SHIVER AS SHE READ THE EMAIL over. Even though they had been emailing regularly for the last couple of weeks, it still made her smile the way Michael signed off his emails as though ending a letter. She was surprised he didn't write the date and his address at the top.

Aside from the picture of the young boy, she had no idea what he looked like. If he cared to check her profile he would see a couple of dozen pictures of her in various situations, some alone, some with work friends, some with Steve. She hadn't taken the old pictures down, because every time she went to do it, it felt like she was showing a little too much intent, that she really was starting to get feelings for a blank profile picture and a few polite words. And plus, if he thought she was with someone, it would make him talk more freely, not trying to impress her—

(Lily, pack it in)

She gave her cheek a light slap, closed her browser, then immediately opened it again when she realised she hadn't replied. Her fingers trembled as she started to type.

Dear Michael, it was lovely to hear from you again—

'Delete,' she muttered.

Hey Michael, thanks for—

'Delete!'

Michael—

She closed the browser again, gripped the side of her face with her hands and tried not to growl, howl, snarl, or make any other kind of animal noise that might disturb Uncle Gus and Aunt Gert from the game of Risk they were currently halfway through.

She was working until five today, although, as she had discovered over the last few weeks, when there wasn't much to do, Uncle Gus and Aunt Gert were quite happy for her to hang around the place and do her own thing, on the off chance that someone rang up or a guest arrived.

'You know those scones that Jimmy's mother dropped round?' she said, poking her head into the restaurant. 'I was thinking of taking a couple down to Victoria. Can you handle the phones?'

Uncle Gus didn't look up from the game, but lifted a hand and gave her a thumbs' up, which she took as an affirmative. Smiling at Uncle Gus's grim expression as Aunt Gert sat back in her chair, chuckling to herself, Lily went into the kitchen and prepared a spread of afternoon tea for Victoria: some scones, a couple of rounds of tuna and cress sandwiches, some French Fancy cakes, and then threw in a wholegrain blueberry muffin just for a little healthy balance.

A few brittle leaves fluttered across the path as she cycled down to the annexe, the afternoon sun turning the line of willow trees into mottled explosions of autumn colour. Lily parked her bike outside, then went around to the annexe's rear and set out a picnic blanket on the grass she had cut a couple of days before. Then, leaving the hamper outside, she went into the building and upstairs to knock on Victoria's door.

Her initial knock was unanswered, so Lily frowned as she lifted her hand to knock again. She had never tried to coax Victoria outside during the afternoon before, but figured that if her attempts failed, she could always carry on down the cycle path and pick a random fisherman to treat to an afternoon picnic.

Just as she went to knock once more, the door flew open, and Victoria appeared, dressed in an elegant beige coat that reached to her knees. She looked like the lead in a cozy mystery series, the kind set in rural villages just like Willow River. So initially shocked did Lily feel, that she almost forgot to stop her hand before it struck Victoria's nose.

Luckily Victoria didn't seem to notice as she breezed past Lily into the hall without a word, sauntered to the end of the corridor before she turned back and said, 'Belinda, are you coming?'

Lily smiled. 'Right away, Madam.'

'I saw you from the window,' Victoria explained outside, as she set herself down on the ground with little of the grace with which she had left her room. 'I must admit,

I wondered at all the activity the other day, so I've been keeping an eye on things. I can't believe you had all this cut because of me.'

'I was thinking of putting a few picnic benches in,' Lily said. 'There are a couple at the front that the council put in, but this would make a lovely rest spot along the cycle path, I think. If Uncle Gus agrees, we could also put some play equipment up. You know, for kids.'

'Well, I don't think I'll be crossing the monkey bars any time soon,' Victoria said, looking around with nervousness. 'Is it really necessary to encourage people to come here?'

Lily shrugged. 'Not much would happen until next year, what with winter on the way. But I was thinking about where to go in my life—'

'Let's talk about the story, dear. Real life scares me.'

Lily rubbed her hands together, then hooked a corner of blanket over her knees. They were sitting in a nice patch of sunlight but the day had taken on that familiar crisp autumn chill, one which reminded Lily of school day evenings, walking home from Mary's house on the other side of the village, hurrying to be home before dark, always jogging, head down as she passed the graveyard behind the church as leaves from the beech trees fluttered across the road and chestnuts fallen from the huge tree on the corner crunched underfoot. She had always taken a moment to pick up any decent sized ones she found, putting them on top of the old stone wall by the church gate, for any boys from the primary school still into playing conkers, all the while avoiding looking across into the graveyard. At the time, balancing a desire to be helpful while not giving in to her fear had been a traumatic ordeal, but through the rose-tinted glasses of nostalgia it had become a fondly cherished memory.

'Are you thinking about it?' Victoria asked, leaning forward to peer into Lily's line of sight. 'The secret?'

Lily, realising she had been gazing off into the distance, gave her head a little shake and then smiled again. 'Maybe. But I can't tell you right away.'

'Why on earth not?'

'Because then it wouldn't be a secret. And a secret can't be revealed until the end, can it?'

Victoria just rolled her eyes and chuckled. 'You'd drive my editor up the wall,' she said. 'She wants to know every twist, every secret, every confrontation up front.' She shrugged. 'Well, she did....'

'Do you ... hear much from her?' Lily asked.

Victoria frowned, and for a moment Lily thought she might open up with something profound. Then she gave a sigh and said, 'So. The story?'

'The girl wants to help the writer come back into the world, so she gradually draws her out of the place she's hiding away in.'

'How?'

'First, she starts making her eat breakfast outside. Then she starts showing up at random times and trying to take the writer out. She wants to go on country walks, go on bicycle rides, and eventually the writer begins to trust her.'

Victoria shook her head. 'We'll have to squeeze that into a couple of chapters,' she said. 'One of the hassles of writing. In a movie they'll do a musical montage with a few snippets showing their growing relationship. In *The Trainspotter's Guide to Romance*, that's the part where Sylvia, the girl, goes crazy learning about trains in order to attract Jack, the boy, finally figuring out where he'll be by which train he'll be working on. That was seven or eight chapters in the book, condensed into three and a half minutes of screen time.'

Victoria sounded a little miffed at this, so Lily spread her hands. 'You could stretch it out if you like.'

Victoria shook her head. 'People have no attention span these days. Books are becoming more like movies day by day. So, what's the big conflict moment that screws up their relationship?'

'When the long-lost son arrives. He shows up, and his mother wants nothing to do with him.'

'And what happens to our heroine? Come on, give me a decent twist here.' Victoria plucked a French Fancy out of its wrapper and popped it, whole, into her mouth. 'We need something a little dramatic, but not too much. Maybe a brief tissue moment. What have you got for me?'

'The son wants to leave, but the girl convinces him to stay, setting up a meeting. However—' Lily couldn't help but grin, '—she finds she really likes him, and something happens between them. They fall in love and get married.'

Victoria looked up. 'That's it?'

'It has a happy ending.'

'So? It's boring. And what happens to the writer? Does she jump off a cliff or throw herself under a bus, allowing them to unite in their grief?'

'I thought you were writing a rom-com?'

'It's okay if someone dies if it advances the plot.'

'What about if the writer just pretends to die?'

'Is that our secret?'

Lily shrugged. 'It could be.'

'Well, it isn't now, because you just told me. You need to come up with another one.'

'Give me a minute. Shall we have a cup of tea? It's lovely out here, but it's getting a little chilly.'

They carried on eating in silence for a few minutes, enjoying the gentle sway of the willows and the last sun as it dipped towards the western hills.

'So, Victoria,' Lily began, hoping now was the right time for a pry. 'Do you have children? You mentioned someone called Michael—'

'It's getting a little cold, isn't it?' Victoria said, not looking at Lily, but leaning awkwardly forward and then standing up. 'I think we should perhaps call it a day, or an afternoon, or whatever you say at the end of these things.'

'I'm sorry, I didn't mean to be nosey—'

'—and I have plenty to go on for now. It's your day off tomorrow, isn't it? I shall so miss you.'

'Thanks, but—'

Too late, Victoria had gone, heading back across the grass and into the annexe, leaving Lily to clear up. With a frustrated sigh, Lily watched her go.

22

TREES AND INSURANCE

'UNCLE GUS, WOULDN'T IT BE BETTER IF I CLIMBED UP the ladder?' Lily asked, afraid that should the ladder give way, Uncle Gus would come tumbling down to crush her like a giant human landslide. 'It feels a bit rickety—'

'A real man is never afraid to get his hands dirty,' Uncle Gus called over his shoulder, briefly leaning backwards, the ladder flexing. Lily, heart in her mouth, feared she was about to experience a moment straight out of a slapstick movie, and glanced over her shoulder to see where he was likely to land.

Right on top of a stone statue of a fox in the middle of a ring of bushes: ouch.

'Please be careful up there—'

'Don't worry, I've done this a million times,' Uncle Gus said with a chuckle, reaching up and scooping a handful of leaves out of the drainpipe and attempting to deposit them into a bucket hanging on a hook by his side. While some made it, others didn't, showering Lily with a cascade of wet, decomposing leaves. She managed to duck away from some, but one struck her right in the middle of the forehead.

'There are people you can hire to do this kind of thing.'

'It's just this little bit where that sycamore hangs over. I should cut it back, but it's a pretty tree, isn't it? I remember you climbing up there and getting stuck once. I was all ready to start hauling the old mattresses out of the shed so you could jump, but someone went up and got you.'

Lily frowned, the ghost of an old memory slinking into focus. She hadn't thought about that day in years, but now that she did....

'I was trying to spy in through an upstairs window,' she said, smiling. 'There was that guy off children's telly staying and I wanted to spy on him. Oh my god, I haven't thought about that in ... years.'

'Andi Peters,' Uncle Gus said. 'He was opening the new restaurant up at Wright's. 'You kids were thrilled.'

'I got his autograph in the end,' Lily said, the memory flowing back like a river into a dry lake bed. 'He signed my old Barbie Annual because that was all I could find.'

'You were stuck in that tree for ages,' Uncle Gus said with a chuckle, dropping another handful of leaves in the general direction of the bucket, making Lily duck to avoid another cascade of gunky leaves. 'We thought you'd never get down.'

'Who was it who got me down? Dad?'

'It was some kid. I don't remember his name now. The son of one of the guests. You were always over here in the summer, playing with the kids staying at the guesthouse. We had a lot of regulars, and you all knew each other. It was one of them, I expect.'

'It was ... oh, god.'

'No, it definitely wasn't him,' Uncle Gus said, as he started to climb down the ladder. 'That lazy old sod might have sent down a lightning bolt or whatever, but I can't imagine he'd go to the trouble of climbing up a tree.'

Lily remembered now. The little boy in the photograph.

'Michael,' she said, as Uncle Gus reached the bottom of the ladder, then jumped down the last two steps, making it wobble and threatening to overbalance the whole thing.

'You mean, Vicky's boy?'

'Yes.'

Uncle Gus shrugged. 'I suppose it could have been. All looked the same to me. Right, that's a job well done. Just got one more spot to do round the back.'

'I think I'm falling in love with a ghost,' Lily said, looking at her parents across the dinner table, a couple of glasses of wine having loosened her tongue.

'Well, probably better than falling for a human,' Sarah said, giving Pete a wry grin. 'I imagine they smell better. As in, not at all.'

'And eat less on dates,' Pete said. 'Got to save your pennies when you can. Which ghost will this be, out of interest? Not old Harry, who haunts the bridge down by the Moor Cross tunnel?'

'Who?'

Pete laughed. 'Don't worry, I made him up. Are we going to have to guess?'

'Dad, do you remember when I got stuck up the sycamore tree up at the guesthouse, and Michael Borton climbed up and helped me down?'

Pete shrugged. 'Vaguely. I was at work. I remember Angus mentioning it offhand once or twice, but it wasn't a big deal. You were only up there for five minutes.'

'That's not what he said.'

'Ah, you can't have been more than eight or nine. I imagine you kids got up to way worse than that. Do you remember the time you and Mary fell in the river and the police came out?'

Lily grimaced. 'I was seventeen, and Colin's older brother had been sneaking us drinks in The Crown's beer garden. We stole a canoe and then capsized it. I remember the policeman laughing.'

'You were such a tearaway in your teens,' Sarah said. 'I thought you were heading for a life of crime.'

'I wasn't that bad,' Lily said, remembering a couple of other drunken escapades, and feeling glad her parents had no idea what she'd got up to at university. 'Do you remember much about Michael?'

'The boy?' Pete shook his head. 'Not really. Angus and Gert used to look after a bunch of you while we were at work. We'd send you over in the morning and pick you up in the afternoon. Most of the time you'd just play out on the grass outside, or go through Angus's stack of board games if it was raining. It helped us out a lot.'

'Do you remember me playing with Michael?'

Pete shrugged. 'I wouldn't have known any of their names.'

'Actually,' Sarah said, leaning forward. 'I think I do. I picked you up a few times, and there was always a boy about. Sweet little thing. A little … weedy. Like he'd end up selling insurance or something.'

'Selling insurance … right.'

'And he was always sick. His mother would come running over with a tissue as soon as he started sniffing, grab the back of his head with one hand and squeeze the tissue over his nose with the other, like she was trying to put him out for an operation or something.'

'His mother … did you ever talk to her?'

Sarah shrugged. 'Not really. Didn't really get a chance. She wasn't particularly conversational. The boy seemed nice. Always polite. A shame he always looked either sick or about to get sick. And his sleeves were always crusty from wiping away the snot.'

'Grim.'

'So, is this boy the ghost you're talking about? Did he die or something?'

Lily shook her head. 'No, I think he's still alive. Unless ghosts have learned how to use computers.'

She decided to go to bed before she could embarrass herself any more, but alone in her room she opened her laptop, pulled up her social media and stared at Michael's latest message. His profile picture was unchanged, just a blank circle, and when she clicked on his profile page there was nothing to display except a few uninteresting memes. His friend list was hidden and he had no pictures to display.

'So,' Lily whispered. 'You're weedy, always sick, and probably an insurance salesman. Not so promising, is it?'

Still, she was drunk enough to type a quick message.

Dear Michael,
I tried to ask Victoria about you today, but she deflected my attempt.
Did something bad happen between you? I think it might help if you
could come up and see her. Can you take time off from your insurance
job?
Kind regards,
Lily

She sent the message before she could chicken out, wondering if the deliberate mention of insurance would compel him to correct her. No one would want to be associated with a job in insurance unless that really was their job. Surely some time tomorrow he would respond, telling her that—

A message flashed up in the box. Lily stared. He was still awake, and had replied.

Her hands shook as she opened it.

Hi Lily,
Thanks for your message. I'll see what I can do. It sounds like she doesn't want to see me. Thanks for trying. I should be able to come up soon, if all goes well. I really appreciate you being so kind to my mother.
By the way, it's pretty late. You should get to bed!
Thanks,
Michael

The message was just as mature as the others, without any of the silly emojis or punctuation characters she sometimes got even from her old workmates. And Michael sounded so kind … Lily slid down in the bed, her laptop on her tummy as she swooned at the ceiling, then abruptly forced herself to sit up. She was being an idiot; she wasn't sixteen anymore, and he hadn't corrected her on the insurance thing, so her mum's guess must have been true. However, telling her she should go to bed had been a little let down of the formality guard he had hitherto kept in place.

If he could do it, so could she.

Michael, I hope I didn't wake you up! You're right, I should get to bed. By the way, do you remember a little girl you rescued from a sycamore tree outside the Willow River Guesthouse? It must be fifteen years ago now. That was me.
Lily

She sent the message, then immediately regretted it. They had been so formal, but now she had crossed the line into borderline flirtatiousness. She didn't even know what he looked like now. He could be thin and weedy or the size of a house. He might be bald, or cross-eyed, or walk with a limp. Not that she believed she was shallow, of course, but a boyfriend was about a total package. You could be mates with anyone, and she liked Michael's personality enough that she would be mates with him even if he had an elephant's nose, three legs, and farted when he walked, but she wouldn't want to go out with him. After her experience with Steve, she had found herself craving some kind of relationship, one that was more than downing tequilas in the pub or throwing high-fives after a skittles strike.

No reply. She really had pushed it too far. Even if he looked like a TV actor, there was no way she had a chance now. She had crossed the line—

A message appeared, and Lily was so desperate to open it that she nearly dropped the phone.

Hi Lily,
Yes, I remember that day. I hoped it was you.
Goodnight,
Michael

23

VISITOR

IN ORDER TO CLEAR OUT SOME OF THE FUNK THAT WAS starting to cloud her thoughts, Lily caught the bus into Brentwell on Wednesday morning to do a bit of shopping, distancing herself from the guesthouse, Victoria, Michael, and all the strange events and possibilities that were beginning to swirl like freshly made coffee around her. She had been tempted to bring her laptop but in the end had decided to leave it at home, but as she wandered up and down the high street, briefly looking around a couple of the newer shops, all she could think about was getting home and replying to Michael. She was starting to lose herself again, and she mentally scolded herself, remembering how it had been at the beginning with Steve, endless text conversations whenever they weren't together, analysis of every word and every pause before a reply. She hadn't really felt sure about their relationship until he had proposed, as though that ring on her finger had been the certificate of companionship that her fragile confidence had needed. Before it happened, she had pestered him about moving in together, only to be constantly rebuked by his requirement of a studio and personal space for his art.

Now, of course, she knew why.

As she walked up and down the street, she couldn't help but glance at the people she passed, wondering how closely they would fit into the mould she had mentally built for Michael. What if that was him, with the beard and the nose ring, or was that him, the man whose cheekbones were so hollow he had to subsist off lettuce and water, or that hulking guy with the bulging muscles?

She stood and stared for a long time at a man in a black suit with a clipboard under his arm, knocking on the door of a townhouse, his hair neatly cropped, clean shaven, spectacles perched on his nose. The man fit her image perfectly, especially when he gave a little cough into his sleeve, and Lily tried to force an attraction, just in case this was him, this was Michael—

'Jim Swift from South West Water,' the man called, leaning close to the door. 'I'm just calling around to see if you're interested in having a new immersion heater installed….'

Lily sighed and moved on.

She didn't really buy much in the end; a sweater, some new tights, and a cheap pair of trainers in an autumn sale, but as she drove back to Willow River, she felt a sudden pang of loneliness. Aside from a few brief messages, she hadn't been in contact with any of her old London friends in the weeks since moving home. Life moved fast in the city, and they had likely moved on. Her desk at Davidson's had been refilled, and she was fast fading into obscurity. Wanting some kind of human contact, she got off the bus outside the church and headed over to the coffee shop, where she caught Mary just finishing up her shift.

'Hello, stranger. How are you doing?'

'Got time for a quick coffee? Or I can walk with you over to the school if you like.'

'No probs. The boys have got a practice thing for the harvest festival next week. They're doing some little stage play so I don't have to get them until half four. You look all flustered. What's going on?'

Lily shrugged. 'I don't know. I guess I'm feeling this kind of weirdness about everything.'

'Sounds like you need a night out.' Mary chuckled. 'If you can hang on six to eight months, until I've got this one out and on the bottle, we'll get a movie night going on.'

'Sorry, I didn't mean to be all needy when you're there with two—and soon three—kids.'

Mary shrugged. 'Don't worry about it. I'll tell you one thing—once you've got a kid or two running around your feet, you learn the value of free time. Get half an hour to yourself and it's like gold. Don't waste a second of it.'

'All right, I'll try.'

'Get down the pub, get out to the shops, get yourself a business going if that's your thing. Once you've got kids—and I wouldn't change anything for the world—getting five minutes just to put your feet up becomes a nearly impossible challenge.'

'I don't think I'm likely to have kids any time soon.'

'Ah, you're still young. But you never know when someone could come into your life and sweep you off your feet.'

The coffee pot had finished brewing, so Mary poured out a couple of cups and they sat down at a table.

'So, can you work your fortunetelling magic on me and tell me when that's likely to happen?' Lily said. 'Because I've kind of given up.'

Mary smiled. 'It could be sooner than you think. You

never know, when you get home tonight there could be someone special waiting for you.'

'I'll cross my fingers, but I doubt it.'

'You've always got to have hope.' Mary chuckled. 'I know there's slim pickings in the village—I pretty much lucked out with Andy—but you're working over at the guesthouse now, aren't you? Don't you get any handsome guests staying?'

'It's mostly middle-aged couples or elderly folk,' Lily said. 'I'm keeping my eye out for a rich sugar daddy, though.'

'That's the spirit.'

They talked for a while, the conversation coming easier as the time passed. Having felt so disjoined when she had first met Mary again, fearing that their lives had diverged too much to ever rekindle their friendship, she realised not so much had changed after all. Now that she was home, slipping back into the world they had once shared together, she began to feel hope that their friendship might bloom again.

'I'd be happy to babysit if you and Andy ever want to go out,' Lily said. 'I mean, you'd have to walk me through the steps in keeping children alive and contained, but it can't be that hard, can it?'

Mary laughed. 'I'll hold you to it. Perhaps in another eighteen months. But once the little one's out, I'd be delighted if you could come over and hold her for a couple of hours while I sleep.'

'Sure, any time. Her? Do you know?'

Mary smiled. 'I just have a feeling this one's a little girl. Although I wouldn't mind another little boy. Once you start, you can never have enough. Talking of which, I'd better head over to get the first two.'

Lily felt much more buoyant as she headed for home.

Mary had a warmth about her that just made her feel better, and she promised herself that she would stop by the café more often. As for her prediction, though, Lily found herself smiling as she crossed the bridge over Willow River and headed up the hill towards her parents' house. How nice it would be to find someone waiting for her, but she sincerely doubted it—

An unfamiliar car was parked outside her parents' place, on the grass verge just back from the gate. A hire car sticker was peeling in one corner of the windscreen. Perhaps Michael had hunted down her address, but was nervous about bumping into Victoria at the guesthouse, and had come here instead. As Lily headed up the path to the house, she felt so nervous she wasn't sure if she would be able to speak.

'Mum? Dad?' she croaked, opening the door and peering into the hall. A pair of shoes she didn't recognise stood on the mat, beside the shoe rack where her parents' kept their shoes. Size nines, there was a speck of something on them which seemed to cut out Lily's heart even before she realised what it was. She started to back away, the enthusiasm dropping out of her as though she were a bag of stones with a hole ripped in the bottom.

Too late, the door into the living room opened, and Pete stepped through, a grim expression on his face.

'Lily, he's here.'

She tried to get out of the front door, but it had shut and her hands missed an attempted scrabble for the handle, leaving her pawing at the closed door like a dog trying to get out.

Flecks of paint.

Of course.

He appeared behind her dad, a longing, puppy-dog

look on his face that she had once found so endearing, but now wished she had the strength to slap away.

'Lily,' Steve said, cocking his head, his eyebrows drooping, a pout on his face that suggested he might start to cry, 'I know I'm the last person you probably want to see, but can we talk?'

24

—————

HEART TO HEART

HER MUM AND DAD HAD GONE OUT INTO THE GARAGE, Sarah ostensibly offering to help Pete finish his latest mural, leaving Steve and Lily alone. Her mum had already made Steve coffee, Lily resenting every sip he took as he sat across from her, spinning line after line like an overzealous spider. She wanted to get angry, but she just felt deflated, empty. As she sat in near silence, listening to him make his excuses, she wished she could just dissolve into the floor.

'I was just feeling lost,' he said with a long sigh. 'You were always so busy with work, and I was craving attention. It was childish, foolish, but it's my sensitivity which allows such things to happen. I never meant to hurt you.'

So, it was her fault he had found another woman. There was a surprise. It was also her fault that he'd failed to sell anything, because her lack of enthusiasm had sucked away his creativity. No mention of course, that her money had given him the freedom to do what he liked without ever needing to worry about getting an actual job.

'I mean,' Steve said, giving a dry chuckle and shaking

160

his head. 'Us creative types, we're so fragile. We're like bits of paper really. So easily broken. I tried to toughen up, but every time you went to a work meeting or some function, I felt like I was being rejected.'

Lily could count on one hand the number of times she had gone to any work-related event outside of scheduled hours over the three years she had lived and worked in London. It would have taken her a few dozen hands however, to count the number of times she had rushed out of her office at lunchtime and hurried over to Steve's studio, just to spend twenty minutes eating a sandwich together.

'I didn't want to feel that way, because I knew you were busy with your *financial* job....'

The way he stressed the word "financial", as though Lily had in some way done something wrong by not being an artist or a writer or a poet or a street musician standing in a cold Underground station somewhere, slowly began to fill her resolve with a sense of anger. Rather than rage at him, however, she could only remember the good times they had spent together, and how his betrayal had left her feeling empty, as though the carpet of a joyful and wondrous future had been pulled out from under her.

'But despite everything, I'm sure we can work this out,' Steve was saying, his voice taking on a drone that Lily was slowly filtering out.

'Steve—' she began, ready to finally cut him off for good, but he put up a hand and shook his head.

'Don't. Let me finish what I have to say. I did it, Lily.'
'Did what?'

'I got that big commission we were dreaming of. The refurbishment of Lemon Street Underground Station, they want to use my art in the redesign. I got a contract last week. It'll be a year's worth of work, but the money ... it's unbelievable. And it's not just that, but I get complete creative freedom. It's everything I—we—hoped for.'

'Well, ah, congratulations.'

'Despite having to move studios at such short notice,'—Lily didn't miss the little dig, but Steve was staring at the space between his wildly gesturing hands like a conjurer magicking up a future—'I managed to pull it off. And from here, who knows where things will lead? You know, so much of my … confusion … was over what was going to happen in the future, but now that's ironed out, I can move on from those troubled times. I can move on … with you.'

'What are you talking about?'

'I'm sorry for everything,' Steve said. 'I want you to come back to London. This time things will be different. We can get another, bigger flat. I'll still need my studio, of course, but we—'

'What do you mean, "we"?'

'You always wanted to live together, didn't you? Well, now that I have a clear focus, I can handle someone else in my personal space. As long as you respect my work, I don't know why we can't make another go of things.' He leaned across the table and put his hands over Lily's before she could pull them away. In that moment she felt that old familiar thrill, the one she had loved so much, and despite the arrogance in his words that was beating on the side of her head like a big fat gong, so much of her wanted to believe him, to go back to London and to rebuild her dreams of marriage and a future with Steve, glue the shards together like one of her father's murals.

Very gently, she pulled her hands away from his and stood up.

'I can't … this is too sudden … I have to think,' was the best she could do. Her heart wouldn't let her utter an outright rejection, but putting some space between them felt appropriate.

'I'm sorry,' Steve said, standing up. 'I shouldn't have been so forward so soon. I'm staying nearby for the next couple of days, and you have my number. I'll call you tomorrow afternoon if I don't hear from you before then. Just think about what I said.'

He went out of the room, and a few seconds later the front door closed with a soft thud. Lily closed her eyes and waited until she heard his car engine starting up, then she went into the kitchen, opened the cupboard and pulled out a bottle of red wine.

The door leading out to the garage opened and her dad came in, her mum at his shoulder, both peering at her expectantly.

'Everything all right?'

Lily shook her head. 'No.'

Pete came forward, arms opened to wrap her into a hug, but right now, she needed to be alone with her confusion. She backed off, shaking her head.

'I'm going for a walk,' she said.

'Are you sure you're not going to do anything stupid?'

Lily shook her head. 'Absolutely not. I just need some air.'

'At least take a corkscrew and a glass,' Sarah said, opening a draw with one hand and a cupboard with the other.

Lily smiled. 'Thanks, Mum.'

'If you're not back by ten I'll call the police,' Pete said.

'Dad, I'm twenty-six.'

'All right, eleven.'

Lily nodded. 'I'll do my best.'

She gave them both a quick hug, then headed for the door, the bottle of wine, a glass, and a corkscrew conveniently placed in a plastic bag her mum had provided. It was only just past dinner time, but the nights were already getting shorter, and what light was left in the day would soon fade, bringing with it the evening chill, so Lily pulled on a thick coat, taking a hat and scarf with her, just in case.

Outside, she wasn't sure what to do, so she walked down the road to the bridge over the river, and then down the steps onto the cycle path. The sun was low in the sky, soon to set behind the distant hills, its deep reds and oranges filtering through the changing leaves of the willow trees alongside the river, leaving the cycle path a mottled contradiction of shadow and colour. Lily didn't want to risk being seen from the guesthouse, so she wandered down towards the annexe, looking for a good spot to sit and toast her sorrows. About halfway there she spotted a nice place under the trees, but the grass was wet, so instead she carried on, aiming for one of the council picnic benches on the riverside outside the annexe.

To her surprise, one of them was already occupied, a figure dressed in a thick duffel coat, the hood pulled up. The figure leaned on the table, something in one hand that glinted in the evening sun.

A wine glass. As Lily watched, the figure drained what was left, before producing a bottle from the seat beside them and refilling the glass.

'Hello,' Lily said, walking up to the table. She reached into her bag and pulled out her own wine glass. 'Do you mind if I join you?'

Victoria looked up and gave a soft smile. 'Not at all, dear. I can see you've been crying. Sit down and tell me your woes, and if you don't mind, maybe I'll tell you mine.'

Lily sat down on the wooden bench seat opposite. 'It's

me, Lily,' she said, unsure whether Victoria even recognised her. The writer, however, gave a slow, knowing nod.

'Lily. From the book. I thought it was you.'

'My ex showed up,' Lily said. 'He spun me a line about how he wanted to get back together, how he'd made a bunch of mistakes, blah blah, how it'll be better next time and all that. And you know what? I was tempted. I'm still tempted. Because, despite everything, I loved him. And there's a void in my life that needs to be filled, and he's the closest thing to a decent fit that I can find.'

'There's your internal conflict,' Victoria said, and Lily was more certain than ever that the writer had lost her mind somewhere in the distant past and actually felt like she was living inside a book. 'You know you should walk away, but you can't. But if you go back, sooner or later the same thing—or worse—will happen. And you know it.'

'I do know it.'

'But you don't care.'

'I don't care. Not enough. I gave him my heart, and I let him break it, but I gave it to him so completely that I want him to glue it back together.'

'So that he can break it again?'

Lily shrugged. 'I suppose so.'

'And you know he will. Only next time, it'll be a little more fragile, and it'll break a little more easily. And the time after that, more easily still. Until you're living with a constant, irreparable broken heart. And the sadness will slowly eat away at you, until there's nothing left.'

Lily laughed through a little sob. 'I feel like one of my dad's murals. Like something made up of little pieces of glass.'

'What happens next? What does our Lily do?'

Victoria was talking about the story. As Lily frowned,

Victoria held up her wine bottle, waiting for Lily's glass. Lily held it up and Victoria poured her a generous measure. Taking a slip, Lily said, 'She wants to step away, but she's not strong enough. She can't do it without help.'

'What kind of help?'

'With the writer's wisdom. What happened to the writer?'

Victoria looked down at her hands. The wind rustled through the willow branches, and Lily almost felt like they were crossing a plane between reality and fiction. The sun caught Victoria's face for one last moment, revealing eyes weary from the weight of expectation and some deep, long ago regret.

'The writer made a big mistake,' Victoria said, taking a sip of her wine but not meeting Lily's eyes.

'Her son's father?' Lily said, and this time, the reaction she got was unexpected. Victoria let out a sudden choking sob, clutching her wine glass with both hands like a comfort blanket.

'He was not the mistake,' Victoria said quietly, her voice barely audible. 'But the writer thought he was. The writer, always chasing something else. Something more. Never able to settle for what she had.' Victoria finished the rest of her wine and poured another glass. Her bottle was almost empty, so Lily took out hers and uncorked it while she waited for Victoria to continue.

'He was a simple man,' she said at last, still staring off into the distance. 'Not rich, but not poor, not handsome but not unattractive, but he was kind, and when you spoke his eyes listened, and he understood everything, and he told you all the right things, and he made you feel like you were the most important thing in the world.' She took a deep breath. 'But the writer … she lived in this fantastical world where anything could happen, and she always wanted more. Someone richer, someone more handsome, someone who she felt reached her pompous level of self-importance. And when she started to find success, she started to meet those kinds of people. She did what she wanted, did stupid things, regrettable things, things that the man, the kind, loving man, didn't deserve. And when he walked away, she blamed him, as though it were somehow his fault.'

'He left ... her?'

'Yes. And she made sure she hurt him as much as possible, using her money to take away his only child. But eventually she lost the boy, too. By the time she realised she had made a mistake, she was all alone in the world.'

'What happened to the man? Couldn't she go back and say sorry, tell him she had made a mistake?'

Victoria shook her head. 'It was too late. She had already soured everything, turned him into the mural of broken glass. She could never restore their relationship, but she could say she was sorry, hoping that he could find peace.'

'So did she?'

'He died before she had the chance. A heart attack. He was only thirty-five. And yet she goes on, and on, and on. Living with her regret every day.'

'What about the son?'

Victoria wiped her eyes with a corner of her sleeve, and Lily couldn't help but smile, wondering if that was where the young Michael's habit had come from.

'The son grew up to be an image of the man the writer had thrown away,' Victoria said slowly, sniffing away her tears. 'And when the writer looks at him, she can't see the boy for what he is, but as a representation of what she got wrong.'

'But what if the boy forgives her? He's a different person. Surely the writer has to understand that?'

Victoria nodded. 'Maybe she can, but … she doesn't know how.'

'That's our secret,' Lily said, understanding that within the world Victoria had built around herself she responded better to the fictional part. The reality was too hard to bear. 'The writer's secret is that she made a mistake, one she was unable to ever be forgiven for. But the way she gets through it is by helping Lily not to fall into the same trap. And they develop a bond. Lily helps the writer to overcome her problems, and to understand that she doesn't always need to aim for better. The book that she's writing, for example, it doesn't have to be better than the previous one. Because even if it's not, it can still be good.'

Victoria gave a soft smile. 'Yes, I think that makes sense. But how does the circle close?'

'The circle closes when both the writer and our heroine solve their problems.'

'So, the writer forgives herself, and manages to finish her book, and our Lily moves on from the boyfriend who cheated on her.'

'Yes.'

'But what's the catalyst? The writer isn't strong enough to forgive herself.'

Lily had a moment of clarity. 'The son returns. And he forgives his mother, and she learns to let go of the past, and realise that while he might resemble his father, he's not his father, but a different person.'

'And how does this tie in with Lily?'

Lily realised they'd drunk most of her bottle of wine too, and that she was more than just a little tipsy. The idea of stealing a canoe suddenly seemed like a really good idea.

Might as well push the whole boat out. 'She falls in love with the son,' she said.

Victoria frowned. 'What, you mean, before she's even met him?'

Lily shrugged. 'Why not? It's just a story, isn't it? Anything can happen.'

25

ENDINGS AND BEGINNINGS

When she woke up on Thursday morning, she had a hangover to be proclaimed from the rooftops. After saying goodnight to Victoria, then making sure the woman got back up to her room rather than falling into the river, she had gone over to The Crown for a nightcap, only to step right into the middle of karaoke night. For once, drunk enough to have a go, once Jimmy and his new girlfriend had warbled their way through *I Got You, Babe*, Lily had screeched her way through *My Heart Will Go On*, returning later for an encore of *I Will Survive*, complete with Womble and Colin doing hideous belly-dances from the top of the pool table. When Rick, the landlord, had suggested an after-hours darts tournament, Lily had been unable to refuse, and although she'd lost her winning streak to a lucky bullseye from Martina, she'd had a grand time, one that had well and truly shaken off her somber mood. She made a self-conscious promise to encourage Victoria to come to the next one.

When she finally got up, just before lunchtime, thankful

that it was another day off, she found the house empty but a note on the kitchen table from her dad.

Lily,
Steve's been hanging around outside all morning and rang the house six times before I'd even taken a shower. Can you either tell him to get lost or bury him somewhere? Chainsaw's in the garage and there's a plot behind the fir trees if you need. You'll have to clear the brambles first. Back after lunch.
Love,
Dad x

She picked up her parents' phone, the answerphone machine flashing with missed calls and a couple of voicemails. She made it through the first couple of self-righteous me-me-me's disguised as apologies before getting tired and deleting the rest. She had to do what she had to do, though, so she switched on her laptop and sent him a message to say she would meet him outside the church at three o'clock.

Best to do it close to the graveyard, just in case.

Then, after a couple of coffees and some daytime TV, she checked her social media messages to see if there was anything from Michael, but to her disappointment there was nothing.

Perhaps she should think about giving Steve another chance after all. She stared at a bland lunchtime drama and tried to imagine how life would be, married to an artist. She'd always dreamed of that kind of world, one in which she'd be travelling all over the place, visiting strange and unique places, standing in front of crowds while Steve was applauded at the unveiling of some new masterpiece.

And all the while you'd be financing everything with your suit job, a background fixture while he soaked up all the applause and adoration. And then, after hours, when you were at a business meeting or grooming a new client, he'd be entertaining fans and admirers—

She sat up, nearly dropping her coffee as the front door went and she heard her dad come in, whistling to himself. He put a head through the living room door and frowned.

'You alright?'

'I'm surviving.'

Pete winked. 'Did you can him?'

'I haven't seen him yet, but I'm going to meet him later.'

'Oh, well. Look, you do what's best for you, and your mother and me will support you every step of the way.'

'Thanks, Dad.'

'Right, I'll be out in the garage.'

She tried to concentrate on the TV, but her mind was wandering all over the place, and when a woman in an evening dress slapped a man with slicked hair across the cheek, she couldn't for the life of her remember why. Switching the TV off, she went out into the garden and knocked on the door to the garage.

Pete was inside, already in his overalls, gluing bits of glass to a plywood sheet. He smiled as she came in and sat down on a stood by the door to watch him work.

'So, Dad, is that like, a metaphor for self-consciousness, or an expression of confusion?'

Pete looked at her and frowned. 'Ah, no. It's a giraffe. I haven't done the head yet, which is probably why you're confused. This is a draft for the wall of the new enclosure at Exeter Zoo.'

'I didn't know Exeter had a zoo.'

'It doesn't … yet. It's opening next year. Big secret. I got a commission to do three of these. The real thing will be about ten foot high.'

'That's great.'

Pete shrugged. 'It is what it is.'

'You must feel proud, though, to see your stuff displayed for everyone to see.'

'That's the best part.'

'I wish I could do something artistic.'

'Why don't you?'

Lily shrugged. 'I don't know what I can do. All I've ever been good at is making small numbers into bigger numbers.'

'Ah, but art doesn't just mean painting or sticking bits of glass on a wall. It can come in all forms. Ask Jimmy up at the farm shop how he feels putting his fruit and veg on display, stuff he's grown himself. I know exactly how he'll feel. Proud.'

'So you think I should grow something?'

'I think you need to find your place in the world. That's all. But you're still young. There's no hurry. Why don't you go overseas for a bit, do some travelling?'

'Are you trying to get rid of me?'

'Of course not. But sometimes you need to step outside the box in order to see what you like about the box.'

'I'm not sure that makes sense.'

Pete chuckled. 'Me neither.'

The time was creeping away, so Lily left Pete to his mural and went to meet Steve. As she walked down the hill and across the bridge, she felt like a teenager on the way to some schoolyard confrontation. Picking a leaf out of the hedgerow, she pulled off small bits at a time, repeating, 'Dump him, forgive him, dump him, forgive him,' over and over. When she ran out of leaf, she picked another, and continued, expanding her options a little:

'Dump him, forgive him, slap him, set fire to him, bury him, steal money from him, hide from him, steal a car and run away with him—'

'Excuse me? I'm sorry to bother you, but I'm trying to find Willow River Guesthouse.'

Lily looked up and blinked. A young man stood in front of her, a rucksack slung over his shoulder a little out of place against the smart-casual suit jacket he wore over jeans. He had a hint of beard and wore glasses. His hair was neatly cut, his smile warm, brown eyes the colour of hot chocolate brimming with intelligence as he watched her, his head slightly cocked.

'I didn't mean to startle you,' he said.

Lily stood frozen to the spot, unable to move. His voice … it was deep and calming like one of her mother's motivational CDs, the kind of voice she could lose herself in. She made a mental note to tell Victoria to—to—to—

'Are you alright? I do apologise if I disturbed you.'

He was a little taller than her, perhaps six foot, his shoulders wide, the shirt under his jacket tight around the waist. While he lacked the muscle of a bodybuilder, he looked like he jogged or spent hours walking each day.

Lily tried to pull her eyes away but failed.

The man chuckled. 'I can ask up the street if you'd prefer. I passed a café—'

'Guesthouse,' Lily finally managed to say, lifting a hand and pointing at the guesthouse, clearly visible halfway up the hill a little further along the valley, although her tongue didn't move properly, and the word came out more like, 'Gowse.'

The man smiled, and Lily felt her knees go weak. She needed to sit down soon before she passed out. He was wearing something too, some kind of aftershave, not enough to be intrusive but just enough to be noticeable.

'Wow, so close,' the man said. 'I can't believe I didn't see it. I think I must have my map upside down. Thank you very much for helping me.'

Lily managed to nod. She looked around, wondering where the man had come from, then noticed a bicycle leaning against the wall of the bridge on the other side of the road. It was an expensive one, with bags on either side of the back wheel and a storage box behind the seat.

'Bike,' she said, managing only a weak nod.

'I cycled down from Exeter,' the man said. 'It was a lovely ride. Do you live around here?'

Lily nodded back over her shoulder as though to indication the direction of her parents' house. The man just smiled again.

'Well, I guess I'm going up the hill. You looked like you were going up the hill, too. If you give me a moment to get my bike, we can walk together.'

Lily felt all shivery inside. She couldn't remember the last time she'd felt this way, perhaps if ever. Her heart was thundering like one of the trains that had once passed beneath this bridge, her cheeks were smarting and her tongue felt dry. As the man crossed the road to get his bike, briefly turning those delightful eyes away from her, she gave her cheek a little slap, trying to get a hold of herself.

He collected his bike, waited for a moment as a car passed, then crossed back over.

'This is a beautiful little village,' he said with a smile. 'You know, I came here a few times when I was young, but I haven't been back here in several years. It looks so different now. My name's Michael, by the way.'

Lily felt like she was sitting on the ground and looking up at a towering cliff as she reached out to take Michael's offered hand. His palm felt warm, his fingers strong.

'Lily,' she said. 'Lily Markham.'

Michael smiled, and a hint of red appeared in his cheeks. 'Lily. I thought it was you. I'm so happy to see you again.'

26

CHILDHOOD MEMORIES

It took a couple more minutes, but Lily eventually recovered the ability to speak in normal, rational sentences. Michael, however, upon learning of her identity, seemed to develop the same affliction with which she had initially suffered, stumbling over his words as though his previous rationality had deserted him.

'I feel like we almost know each other already,' Lily said, trying not to gush as she recovered her voice. 'I mean, we were friends as kids, weren't we?'

Michael nodded. 'Kids. I … really—'

'You rescued me from that tree.'

'Tree? Oh, I—'

'And I just remembered—' Lily laughed. 'Sorry, I really should shut up.'

'It's okay,' Michael said.

'Perhaps we should just take a deep breath,' Lily said. 'Maybe count to ten or something.'

'Okay.'

Lily watched him as she counted on her fingers. His

eyes never left hers. At eight she started to laugh. He lifted an eyebrow and began to laugh too.

'No wonder time passes so quickly here,' he said. 'That wasn't ten.'

'It worked, though, didn't it?'

Michael looked around him, then smiled. 'I think it did. I'm Michael. Did I tell you that?'

'Yes, you did.'

'Thank you for getting in contact with me. Really, thank you.'

'It was my pleasure. Your mother … she seems kind of sad. I just wanted to help her out a bit.'

'It sounds like you did. And you helped me, too.'

'Did I?'

Michael nodded. 'I needed an excuse to come back. It's been too long.'

'Willow River?'

Their painstaking progress had taken them across the bridge, where another set of steps led down to the cycle path. Lily headed that way without thinking, then realised Michael had his bike. She looked back to see him carrying it over his shoulder with relative ease.

'Sorry, it's just I usually go this way. Up the path a little and then cut across the meadow outside the guesthouse. It's quicker.'

'Works for me.'

'Isn't that heavy?'

'A little, but I can manage.'

Lily hurried down the steps, then waited at the bottom for Michael to come down. She reached out to help him with the rucksack that was dangling loose from his shoulder, her arm briefly touching his. She shivered, then immediately scolded herself for being such a teenager. She held the bag while he put the bike down, then held it out as he turned around.

'Thanks,' he said.

They sat down on a bench near the river without even thinking about it, Michael leaning his bike against one end, then sitting on the river's side while Lily sat on the other.

'I have so many great memories of this place,' he said. 'Life was pretty chaotic when I was a kid, but whenever we stayed here, things seemed to calm down. Are all the old guys still around? Jimmy? Mark? Christina?'

Lily felt a brief pang of jealousy at the mention of her old friend's name, then remembered Christina had moved away when she was nine. A little early for a crush.

'Some,' she said. 'Jimmy works up in the farm shop. 'Mark … I don't know where he went. Christina moved upcountry years back.'

'A lot of people move on,' Michael said. 'I used to dream about coming back here. I always wondered what might have changed. The train being gone … that's the big one. But much of it's the same.'

'And the cycle path is nice.'

'I didn't realise that it was the old train line until I saw the church.'

'Did you come here often?' Lily asked, feeling a little guilty for not remembering better. She was starting to realise how involved she had been during her London years, the intensity of her life pushing her past further away.

'Most summers until I was twelve,' Michael said. 'I went to boarding school after that, then university. I stopped in a couple of times when I was passing through, but then I got busy with work, and you know how it is.'

Lily nodded. 'You start to forget things.'

'I should have thought mother might come back here.

It just felt too obvious.'

'You've had no contact in five years?'

'I get cards at Christmas and on my birthday—well, within a few days—so I knew she was alive. I just trusted her to live her life. And—' His smile dropped.

Lily found herself wanting to reach for his hand, and had to make a conscious effort to keep her own hands on the table.

'What is it?'

'She was never the best mother in the world. It wasn't like she was abusive or even neglectful, she was just … inattentive. I didn't miss her when I went to boarding school, because I'd seen how she treated my father. I kept in touch with her, but I also got back in touch with him, and we had started to meet up, to repair the relationship she had broken. Then he died suddenly, and that was that.'

This time Lily couldn't help herself. She reached across the table, realised too late what she was doing, and settled for putting a hand over his jacket arm instead, as though that were somehow less suggestive.

Michael looked up and smiled but made no move to pull his arm away. Lily's heart almost burst out of her throat as he lowered his own hand over hers and gave it a gentle squeeze.

'I'm sorry,' he said. 'I don't mean to sound like I have issues with my childhood or anything like that. I'm over all of it. It was what it was, and I've reached the stage where I have no hard feelings. I'd really like to repair my relationship with my mother. I was thinking about her a lot, and your message came at exactly the right time. That it was from you, as well….'

He trailed off. His hand was still over hers. Lily gazed at him, wondering what was going on. Was this what it felt like? Was this love at first sight?

'So, tell me,' Michael said. 'What have you been doing these last few years? I gather you're working at the guesthouse these days.'

He gently moved his hand away, and Lily felt like she could breathe again. Even so, it took a couple of breaths to compose herself.

'Only for the last couple of months,' she said. 'I was living in London before that … oh, bloody hell.'

'What?'

Lily grimaced. 'I was supposed to be meeting someone.'

'Really? I'm sorry if I distracted you.'

'No, it's fine.' She stood up. 'I'm sorry, Michael. I have to go. Where are you—can I see you—' She grabbed a handful of her hair and tugged it as though that might shake some sense into her.

'At the guesthouse, and yes,' Michael said, also standing up. 'I'm too scared to approach my mother until you've smoothed the way for me. Until then, I'll just wander around for a bit, perhaps take a photograph or two, then see if the guesthouse has any decent craft ales.'

'Okay, that's great. Lily brushed a couple of leaves off her clothes. 'That's great. Ah, didn't I just say that?'

'You did.'

'Then I'll see you later?'

'Most definitely.'

They stood and looked at each other for a few seconds. Lily was still churning inside, but Michael looked as though he never wanted to look away.

'Right, bye,' Lily said, lifting a hand and giving an awkward flap she hoped would pass as a wave. Then, before she could do something really ridiculous like run over and hug him, she turned and ran for the stairs up to the bridge.

27

CHANGING OF THE GUARD

By the time Lily got to the church, some thirty minutes late, Steve was nowhere to be seen. She glanced over the wall into the graveyard, wondering if he might have taken the hint and buried himself, but the graveyard was empty. Lily paused for a moment to appreciate the primroses planted along the path up to the door, their colour giving a bit of warmth to the field of lichen-covered stones. Then, giving a shake of the head, wondering when she had become so strangely dizzy, she went looking for Steve.

The obvious place was the pub, but inside its dark confines she found only a couple of tourists playing pool. Rick, standing behind the bar, told her he'd seen nothing of an arty-looking guy, but promised to say Lily was looking for him should he come in.

Outside, she wandered down Willow River's small high street, wondering where he might have gone. There was no one in the fish 'n' chip shop, nor in the greengrocers or bakers. She walked past her mother's craft shop, but Delia, her mother's part time assistant, was alone, stringing up some more dreamcatchers in the window.

Finally, she came to the coffee shop, and glancing in the window, found her worst fears realised. Two young girls —Lily guessed they might be university students judging by the designer hiking gear they wore—sat at a table in the corner, while across from them sat Steve, leaning forward, hands gesticulating animatedly as he told them some fanciful tale that, while not keeping them literally on the edge of their seats, certainly had them entertained.

Lily wondered whether she ought to interrupt the party, and was about to push through the door when she saw Steve pull out his phone. The girls responded by pulling out theirs, and in the moment before Steve opened his Whatsapp to collect their contacts, Lily caught a glimpse of his front screen.

While she could hardly have expected otherwise, having previously dumped him—and of course, she had long ago removed her own—but to see that he had replaced the picture of the two of them together moments after getting engaged was like a final stake pushed through the heart of their relationship.

She would call him later. Maybe. She wished she had still had her phone in order to take a photograph just for evidence's sake, but it didn't matter. He wouldn't talk his way out of this one.

None of them noticed her standing there, watching them. No doubt later Steve would try to pass it off as something innocent, that he'd found out they were art students and was giving them a contact in the industry, or perhaps they'd even recognised him from some obscure magazine feature and he had promised—reluctantly, for certain—to secure them tickets for his upcoming exhibition.

Lily knew the drill. But now that she had witnessed Steve in action, there was no going back. She gave a last shrug as though to throw off the shadow he had cast over her, then walked up the street and through the doors of The Crown.

'Did you find him?' Rick asked.

'Yeah, I did,' Lily said.

Rick obviously caught something from her expression. 'Like that, is it? Well, what can I get you?'

Lily smiled. 'Do you have any champagne?'

Rick frowned. 'There might be a bottle out the back. What's the occasion?'

'I'd like to celebrate moving on with my life.'

'Well, there's no better reason to celebrate than that. Just a minute.'

Rick went through a curtain into a back room and reappeared a couple of minutes later with a bottle of Don Perignon.

'Have a glass with me, please,' Lily said. 'And pour one each for those guys over there. Whatever's left please share with the regulars later.'

Rick, chuckling, did as she asked, pouring out four glasses, and calling over the two surprised tourists, who introduced themselves as Lucy Drake and Dan Bale, a couple from Bristol who had recently got engaged.

'I'd like to make a toast to new beginnings,' Lily said, holding up her glass. 'To finding friends in all places, and to following your own true path in life.'

They touched glasses and drank. After a few minutes of genial conversation, Lucy and Dan, who, it turned out, were staying at the guesthouse, made their excuses and headed out, leaving Lily and Rick to finish the last of the bottle.

'I've got another I can put out for the lads later,' Rick

said, 'so don't feel guilty about finishing this one off. Some leftover from a wedding last month.'

'Thanks, Rick,' Lily said, finishing her glass, and feeling happily lightheaded. 'I needed that.'

'So … with all this talk of new beginnings and everything, are you still going to be available for skittles this week?'

Lily frowned. 'If we win, we'll go second in the league, isn't that right?'

'Right.'

'Then I'll definitely be there.'

'Good lass.'

The evenings were drawing in, and the wind was rustling through the trees around the churchyard as Lily headed back through Willow River. As she passed the guesthouse, she thought about stopping in to see Michael, but the day had been a rollercoaster and she needed some time alone to think. She was working tomorrow in any case, so would likely see him then.

The setting sun was glittering off the river as she came to the bridge. She stopped and leaned on the old stone wall, watching a couple of swans gliding serenely through water turned orange and red. The lines of willows on either side shook gently in the breeze, and showers of falling leaves fell across the cycle path with each new gust of wind.

Winter would soon come, but Lily felt more optimistic than she had in weeks. More than anything, she felt free, as though the chains of her old life had finally been shaken off, and the road was clear to make a new start.

Her mum and dad were just sitting down to dinner when she got home a few minutes later.

'Chicken pie,' Sarah said. 'Are you hungry? We weren't sure if you'd be home for dinner or not. How did things go with Steve?'

Lily grimaced. 'Let's just say that I saw a side of him I had long suspected, and it's not something I want in my life. Oh, and I met Victoria's son.'

Pete glanced at Sarah. 'Well … that sounds promising.'

'So, what's he like?' Sarah asked.

Lily smiled. 'He's all right,' she said.

'Is that all right as in all right, or all right, as in, "all riiiiiight!"?'

Lily smiled. 'I can't give you a definite answer yet, because I've only just met him, but let's just say that I'm satisfied with progress.'

Pete opened his mouth to say something else, but Lily put up a hand. 'And anyway, enough about my love life or lack of it. What's news?'

It was clear Pete and Sarah were going to continue to grill Lily for details, so as soon as she was done with dinner, she retreated to her room, lay down on her bed, and opened her laptop.

I waited forever for you today, was Steve's message. *What happened? It hurts to be stood up like that. I thought we were working things out?*

Sarah had poured Lily a glass of wine with dinner, despite Lily's protests. *Nope,* she wrote back, feeling a little combative. *I've had a think about everything, and it's better if we go our separate ways.*

His reply was quicker than she had expected.

I never realised you could be so cold. I made a mistake, that's all.

The wine had definitely gone to her head. *You sponged off me for two years,* she wrote back. *The whole while playing around behind my back. It's me that made a mistake.*

I thought I explained, he replied.

Not well enough. Goodnight, Steve.

She closed his message down, taking a few deep breaths to calm herself. Michael had also messaged her, and she felt in the unenviable situation of feeling both angry and excited at the same time. Taking another breath, she opened Michael's message.

Hi Lily,
The guesthouse is lovely. Like I remembered it and more. Angus's beard is longer than ever, but Gertrude hasn't aged a day! I'm afraid they didn't recognise me, but that's to be expected. Anyway, it's really nice to be back. I haven't tried to contact Mother yet. I was hoping you could help me break the ice tomorrow. You will be in, won't you? I'm really looking forward to seeing you.
Yours,
Michael

There was something about the maturity in the way he wrote that left Lily swooning. She felt like some 19th Century housewife reading mail from her government-employee husband stationed in some far-off land. It was easy to throw off the likely realisms of such a situation and enjoy a romantic view. Separated loves, forced to correspond by long letters delivered by slow-moving paddle steamers. She shook her head as she found herself grinning, but it made no difference.

I'm really looking forward to seeing you too x she typed, then immediately deleted the message before sending.

Come on, Lily, act your age.

'Hi Michael,' she said, dictating the message as she typed, unable to resist putting on a toffy voice. 'Thank you for your message. Yes, I'll be at the guesthouse tomorrow. I hope to see you too.'

She changed it to "really hope", then changed it back. Did it seem too needy, or too forward? In the end, she deleted the last sentence and just wrote "see you then", pressing send before she could stop herself. Immediately after the message had sent, she grabbed her hair and gave it a savage squeeze. That surely wasn't forward enough. He would think she wasn't interested.

She was just starting to type some blathering, vague addendum, when Michael's reply appeared.

Hi Lily, thanks! I'll see you then too.

28

REUNION

'WHAT'S UP WITH YOU THIS MORNING?' AUNT GERT said, handing Lily a stack of bread slices to lie across the guesthouse's industrial-sized grill. 'Were you just whistling?'

'Uh, no.'

'Must be a crack in a pipe somewhere,' Uncle Gus grunted, lifting a large bowl of salad leaves covered with cling film and giving it a savage shake. 'Don't worry, he'll blow soon, and we'll be able to fix him up.'

'No, it was definitely a whistle.'

Lily couldn't keep the smile off her face as she shrugged. 'Perhaps I just heard a catchy song on Uncle Gus's radio.'

'It's to be expected,' Uncle Gus said. 'They're all catchy. The eighties pretty much defined catchy.'

Aunt Gert patted him on the stomach. 'You just keep believing that, dear. It's no different to how you define the perfect man.'

'It's the hair and personality double-combo,' Uncle Gus said. 'Irresistible.'

'I'll take these orders out,' Lily said quickly, fearing that her aunt and uncle might start to kiss. She scooped up the ready plates and carried them through the kitchen doors out into the restaurant. The guesthouse was busy today, the restaurant almost crowded. She delivered the plates to Lucy and Dan, who were sitting by the window. They smiled, then thanked her for the champagne yesterday. As she turned to head back to the kitchen, she found Michael standing right behind her, having just come down the stairs from the guestrooms.

Lily let out a little cry of surprise which made the guests on a couple of nearby tables turn around.

'I didn't mean to startle you,' Michael said, in that soothing voice Lily was certain she had dreamed about. 'Can I sit anywhere?'

He wore only a t-shirt and jeans. His hair was still damp from the shower, but his eyes were bright behind the glasses as though he had enjoyed a solid ten hours of sleep before taking a brisk morning jog along the riverside.

'Yes, anywhere that's free.'

He watched her for a moment, a slight smile on his lips. 'Thank you,' he said at last.

Lily would have been happy to continue staring at him, but Uncle Gus suddenly called her from the kitchen.

'You're welcome,' she muttered, hurrying away, immediately wondering if it was a stupid thing to have said.

'Who's the dish?' Aunt Gert said as soon as the kitchen door had closed behind her, aiming an elbow at Lily's ribs but missing and hitting Lily on the upper thigh instead, making her wince. 'He came in yesterday, didn't he?'

'He gave his name as Michael Hill,' Uncle Gus said. 'Looks vaguely familiar. Perhaps he's a TV weatherman or something. He has that kind of look.'

'He's gorgeous,' Aunt Gert said. 'If I were to update

my rankings with Angus at one, I'd put him probably in the lower top ten, perhaps between George Clooney and that guy who used to present *Top Gear*.'

'Clarkson?'

'No, the other one.'

Uncle Gus just shook his head. 'Haven't seen it in years.'

'That's Victoria's son,' Lily said. 'Hill must be his father's surname. Perhaps he's covering his tracks, to make sure she doesn't find out he's here. Not until he wants her to know.'

'Oh my goodness,' Aunt Gert said. 'I thought he looked familiar. Wow, he's quite the looker. Have you got his number? I can get it off the reservation form if you like. I know that's technically illegal, but who's looking?'

'We've been emailing,' Lily said.

'Oooh,' said Uncle Gus and Aunt Gert together.

'It's not like that.'

Aunt Gert patted her on the arm. 'Well, I'd better get you something to take out to him, just in case,' she said, grabbing a ladle with the other arm and scooping beans out of a pan on to a plate. 'And after you get back, there's a second coffee for that miserable sod on table three. You know, he was moaning yesterday that we should cut the top off the sycamore. Apparently he was expecting to see all the way to Exeter.'

Lily smiled. 'Will do.'

It took all her efforts not to spill food or drink on any of the other guests while she shamelessly tried to watch Michael as much as possible. After sitting down, he had pulled out a paperback book and was making a show of reading it, only looking up a to meet Lily's eyes on five or six occasions, each with a little smile that made her unsure of the ability to walk. When breakfast was over, however, with just Victoria's delivery to do, Lily found him waiting in the lobby area.

'Best toast I've ever eaten,' he said, giving her a smile.

'It took three years of catering college to learn to cook it like that,' Lily said.

'I bet it did.' Michael took a deep breath, then held up a fist. 'I'm ready,' he said. 'Do you think I'll need a motorcycle helmet in case she throws anything at me?'

'Just be ready to grab her if she makes a run for it.'

'Will do.'

She could have taken the bike, but she wanted to talk to Michael as they walked together up the cycle path towards the annexe. Michael, taking one look at the hamper, had insisted on carrying it, although he did allow Lily to hold a separate bag containing a flask and three coffee cups.

'So, what is it you do?' she asked as they walked side by side along the cycle path, red and gold leaves fluttering through the air around them.

'I hassle people who haven't paid their TV licenses,' Michael said.

'Oh.' Lily couldn't help but feel a little disappointed. While she hadn't wanted him to be some mountain explorer or secret agent, there was comfortably boring, and then there was just plain dull.

'Not really,' he said. 'I'm a travel writer.'

'Really?'

He nodded. 'I suppose writing runs in my family, although I'm not famous or anything like Mother is. I do commission work for various guidebooks, a few articles for the BBC, places like that. Mostly UK-based stuff, small town, regional things. I'm actually working on my own book right now, about small town Britain.'

'That sounds awesome.'

'Hence the bike. Most tourists flit through a place in a couple of days, seeing only the main sites, but if you take your time a little, go a little deeper … there's all sorts of interesting things you can learn. Everyone is in such a scramble to be heard these days. Not enough people are prepared to listen.'

Lily nodded. 'Sounds familiar.'

'And what about you? Did you decide to work in the family business?'

He said it without any hint of condescension, as though waiting tables at the Willow River Guesthouse was the most honourable job in the world.

'For now,' she said. 'It's only been a few weeks, though. Before that I was living in London.'

'Really? What did you do there?'

He sounded so interested. Lily found herself talking and talking, starting with the basics, before going deeper, talking about her run of bad luck, Steve, her job, losing her flat, deciding to come back and reset.

Never once did he look bored. He watched her as she spoke, occasionally asking questions to clarify, nodding along and returning comments here and there.

'I'm sorry,' Lily said at last, when she looked up to find they were standing outside the annexe. 'I must sound like one of those talkative types you were saying about.'

'Not at all,' Michael said. 'Sometimes we need to get things off our chest. I think you did the right thing, by the way.'

'With what?'

'With all of it. And take your time before deciding

what to do next. Maybe you'll want to return to the financial sector, or maybe not. There's no rush, though.'

'You sound like a therapist.'

Michael lifted an eyebrow. 'That's too bad. I was hoping I sounded like a friend.'

'You do—I didn't mean—'

Michael put a hand on her arm and laughed. 'Relax, Lily.'

His touch sent a shiver through her, and the way he said her name sent another. Lily felt like she was losing her mind and heart all at once, and part of her wanted to rebel against it.

'Tell me something bad about you,' she said quietly. 'I want to know you're not … not … perfect.'

'Oh, I'm definitely not that,' Michael said with a smile. 'How bad?'

'Really bad.'

'The worst bad of all?'

Lily nodded. 'That's the one.'

Michael's smile dropped. 'This will hurt. Just before I say anything, I want to tell you that I really like you, Lily. I mean, maybe you don't remember but when we were kids I had this weird crush on you, and it's never really gone away. Then when you got in touch with me, it was like a lightning bolt out of nowhere. I never thought I'd ever see you again, but even if I did, there'd be nothing there, I could put my crush back in the cupboard and forget about it, but then I came here and saw you again, and—'

His hand had slipped down her arm and without realising it, Lily found her hand in his. It felt warm, comforting. Natural.

'Just tell the bad thing,' she said.

Michael took a deep breath. 'I'm in a Nickelback covers band,' he said.

Lily almost choked with laughter. 'What? You mean, at university?'

Michael gave a solemn shake of the head. 'No, I mean right now. It's with some other journalists I've known for a while. I play bass.'

Lily took a deep breath. 'So … at least you're not the singer.'

'I was, but we found a better guy.'

Lily nodded. 'And you have … all of their CDs?'

'Digital,' Michael said. 'I can't carry CDs on the bike. But I have an iPod.'

'I'm not sure if we can work past this,' Lily said trying not to smile. 'But maybe we can find you a support group or something?'

'I know it's a deal breaker,' Michael said, 'But I really like them.'

'Uncle Gus will love you,' Lily said quietly. 'Dad too. Mum only listens to opera and new age stuff. Forest sounds, that kind of thing.'

'Are we talking about parents already?'

Lily found herself blushing. 'Oh, I didn't mean—'

Michael squeezed her hand. 'Talking of which … I need to go and see mine.'

Lily gave a little shake of her head. 'I almost forgot. Okay, the plan is, you wait out here. I'll try and bring her down. Stay out of sight until I give a signal.'

'Which will be?'

'I don't know … I'll wave or something.'

'Sounds good.'

'We need to get her outside. That way she can't just lock her door. Right, wait here.'

She reluctantly let go of Michael's hand and took the hamper over to the picnic bench where she had sat with Victoria before. Then, giving Michael a thumbs' up, she headed into the annexe and up the stairs to Victoria's room.

Unable to hide her nervousness, her first knock barely scrapped the wood, so Lily tried again, this time overdoing it and hurting her knuckles. Worried Victoria might think there was some kind of weirdo standing outside her door, she leaned forward and called, 'Victoria? It's just me. Lil … ah, the breakfast girl.'

She waited for a few seconds, but no answer came. She knocked again, but when she still received no answer, she tried the handle and, surprised to find it unlocked, gently opened the door.

Something was off about Victoria's suite. The hallway felt a little different to usual, but it wasn't until Lily crept up to the door to the main room and pushed it open that she really understood.

It was tidy.

Spotless from top to bottom, all the chairs in place, even the bed visible through an adjoining door was neatly made.

And more, it looked as though Victoria had packed to leave. Three large suitcases stood by the door, and remaining in the room were just a few personal items yet to be put away.

Her desk, too, was tidy, cleared of clutter, only the laptop standing open, a cursor blinking on the screen.

Lily put down the hamper and stepped forward, unable to suppress her curiosity.

Victoria had written THE END in bold capitals, beneath a line which made Lily smile.

And they all lived happily … maybe not forever after, but certainly for as long as anyone needs.

The book was done. Lily's immediate thrill was

tempered by her fear for Victoria. What if she had gone and done something stupid now that her work was done?

Lily rushed to the window and looked out, but the meadow behind the annexe was empty. She scanned the tree line of the woodland on the far side, but saw no sign of Victoria there either.

She went back out to the hall. There were several other rooms but Victoria was paying for them all to keep the annexe to herself. Lily tried each door one by one, but they were all still locked.

Hurrying downstairs, she looked in the common areas and the unused kitchen that Uncle Gus had installed, but still saw no sign of Victoria. Starting to worry now, she ran out onto the old platform, and was about to call for Michael when she spotted a figure sitting beneath the willow trees by the riverside.

The floral hat was a giveaway. Lily breathed a sigh of relief as Victoria reached up and ran a hand through the nearest weeping willow branches, plucking a leaf free.

Lily was about to call out when movement to her left caught her eye.

Michael, walking slowly, moved along the riverbank towards Victoria. Lily felt like the only person in a cinema, watching a climatic final scene as Michael lifted a hand to wave as Victoria turned. Over the breeze, Victoria's soft cry of surprise was barely audible as she put a hand over her mouth.

'Hello, Mother,' Michael said as Victoria, tears in her eyes, stood up. 'It's been a long time.'

Victoria said something Lily couldn't hear, then Michael opened his arms and stepped forward, pulling Victoria into a hug. As Victoria, sobbing, buried her head into Michael's shoulder, Lily began to feel a little uncomfortable. Opting to give them their private space, she walked to the end of the platform, down a set of steps to the cycle path, and down on to the riverbank, where she sat on a bench to watch the languid flow of the river. Fallen leaves scattered its surface now, turning it into a flow of orange brown. A pair of swans moved through the water, poking at the leaves as though frustrated they weren't little fish. The breeze was getting stronger, perhaps suggesting a turn in the weather. Lily reached up to rub her shoulders against the cold, and almost cried out as her hand met another hand, reaching down.

'Sorry,' Michael said. 'I didn't mean to startle you.' He rolled his eyes and smiled. 'Um, Marigold, isn't it? Ah, my mother was wondering what happened to her breakfast.'

Lily couldn't help but laugh. 'Yeah, Marigold, that'll do. It's over there, on that picnic table.'

'She said she went for a stroll after finishing her book,' he said. Then, with a grin, he added, 'You were late, apparently.'

'I was distracted.'

'Tut tut. And she says, thank you.'

'Thank you? What for?'

A shadow appeared by Michael's shoulder, and Victoria's face appeared. She frowned, as though being faced with a reality she hadn't known existed. 'For your help, dear,' she said. 'For the book, and for helping me come back to myself.'

Lily smiled. 'All in a day's work,' she said.

29

CONFRONTATION

MICHAEL AND VICTORIA HAD A LOT TO TALK ABOUT, SO Lily left them alone for a while, walking up along the cycle path to the old Moor Cross tunnel, where she stopped to talk to a couple of fishermen sitting by the river. She was gone longer than she had planned, and when she walked back past the annexe at around eleven o'clock, she found Michael sitting alone outside.

'Is everything all right?'

Michael smiled as he stood up. 'It's a work in progress, but we're getting there,' he said. 'She knows I forgive her for whatever happened during my childhood. I don't want to hold grudges, and she's sorry for the way she treated Dad. That's enough for me, and we're going to move forward.' He nodded up at the windows. 'And she's decided to move forward too. Or at least move out. She told me she's got her eye on a cottage on the edge of the village. Do you know the one with the thatched roof on the road to Brentwell? It's up for auction next week, apparently. When my mother isn't writing, she spends a lot of time browsing Rightmove.'

'That place? That's where Christina used to live. It's absolutely gorgeous inside.'

'The current owners only have it as a holiday home, apparently.'

'I bet it'll cost a fortune.'

Michael shrugged. 'I think Mother is sitting on a lot of money. Good luck to her.'

As he looked away, back at the river, Lily felt a sudden lurching in her stomach. Michael had come to reconcile with Victoria, and now that was done—

'Are you … leaving soon?'

Michael looked at her and grinned. 'Leaving Willow River? No. Not right now. I have plenty of other reasons to stick around.' His hand closed over hers. 'I thought I might hang around for a while. Do you think Angus would let you have the afternoon off?'

'To be honest, I don't think he'd notice whether or not I was even there. I'll ask him, though, just to make sure.'

'Great. I want to check out the museum just past the church up there.'

'Seriously? It's tiny and there's hardly anything in it.'

Michael's eyes shone. 'Great. That's exactly the kind of borderline boring place I'm looking for. My readers will love it. And if it's really that rubbish, I'd much rather visit it with company.'

'I'll force myself. Just for you.'

'Thanks.'

They started walking back towards the guesthouse. Lily was positively glowing, Michael walking beside her humming quietly to himself. Everything felt perfect, like a scene from an oil painting—

'Oh, god.'

'What is it?' Michael asked.

Lily stopped. The figure walking along the cycle path

up ahead had spotted her. She felt a sinking feeling in her stomach as Steve, swaying slightly as though he'd already been in the pub, approached, his face creased with anger.

'What's this?'

'Steve? What are you doing here?'

Steve glared at Lily and Michael in turn. 'Just talking a walk. Didn't expect to have it ruined. So what's going on here, then? You run your mouth about me and all this time you're carrying on with someone?'

'It's not like that.'

'Talk about the pot calling the kettle black. You're got a nerve calling me some kind of player when you're doing the same thing yourself.'

'I'm not—' Lily began, but Michael stepped forward.

'Don't speak to her like that,' he said.

Michael had a couple of inches on Steve and was broader at the shoulder. He didn't look like a fighter, but if it came to blows, Michael had an advantage. Lily hadn't realised until now how over Steve she was, but as she looked into his eyes, she felt nothing. Even so, she didn't want to see him get hurt.

'What are you gonna do about it?' Steve said, squaring up to Michael, who still carried the hamper.

'Michael, there's no need,' Lily said.

Then, to her surprise, Michael backed away onto the grass of the riverbank. Steve followed him, eyes hard.

Michael continued to back away, then turned so Steve was on the river side with his back to the water. Then, with a sudden grin, Michael said, 'Catch!'

Steve gasped as Michael tossed the hamper toward him. Steve instinctively reached out for it, but, being filled with crockery, it was heavy. He stepped backward, dropping the hamper on the ground, losing his balance at the same time. One foot slipped, his arms flailed, and he fell backwards into the water.

As Steve splashed about, shouting in anger, Michael reached down and picked up the hamper. He glanced up at Lily, grinned, and said, 'That was unfortunate. I imagine the water's pretty cold.'

Steve had regained his balance and was standing up to his waist in the slow moving water. He glared at Lily and muttered, 'I lost a shoe,' with an angry teenage pout. 'These cost two hundred quid.'

'I know,' Lily said. 'I paid for them. The water's not moving fast. If you feel around a bit, you might find it.'

Steve glared at her a moment longer. Then, scowling, he began to reach into the water like an awkward, unkempt duck. Lily gave Michael's arm a tug.

'Come on, let's go,' she said as they started back along the cycle path, leaving Steve floundering in the water behind them. 'I need to explain these broken plates to Aunt Gert.'

'Just tell her it was windy,' Michael said.

'Windy enough to blow someone into the river? I was worried you were going to hit him there.'

'I've never hit anyone in my life, and I'm not about to start now, but a little swim never hurt anyone. In fact, I've heard a swim in cold water is good for you.' As the wind gusted, showering them with leaves, he added, 'Perhaps we should try sometime?'

Lily laughed. 'Sometime, maybe. But not today. Come on, let's get going, shall we? I've heard that the village museum is so boring that sometimes it just falls asleep and closes itself.'

'Sounds like an interesting place. I can't wait to go. Is your season ticket still valid?'

'What?'

Michael just chuckled. Then, somehow managing to hook the entire hamper under his left arm, he put his right around Lily's shoulders. Despite the wind that was turning colder with each gust, Lily didn't think she'd ever felt so warm.

30

LAST ORDERS

As Lily opened the café door, Mary glanced up and smiled. 'Hello, stranger. Thought you'd come to keep me company on this blustery old day? Honestly, I can't believe it'll be advent calendars next week. Where does the time go?'

Lily smiled, and stepped aside to allow Victoria to come in after her. 'I brought someone for you to meet,' she said, as Victoria pulled off her hat, picked a leaf out of the plastic flowers fed through the ribbon, then gently placed it back on her head.

'Yeah?'

'Mary, this is Victoria,' Lily said, as Victoria looked up and gave a shy smile.

'Hello, dear,' she said.

'Nice to meet you, Vic—' Mary's jaw dropped, and her eyes widened. 'Oh my god. You're not…?'

'I am,' Victoria said, looking a little sheepish.

'She is,' Lily added.

'No way,' Mary said. 'I absolutely love your books. And

Trainspotter' Guide—' She patted her heavily pregnant belly. '—me and the soon-to-be watch it all the time.'

'Well, thank you....'

Victoria still looked awkward, but Lily took her arm and guided her forward. 'Don't worry, it'll get easier with practice,' she whispered. Then, to Mary she said, 'Victoria's just bought Sycamore Cottage. You know, where Christina used to live.'

'No way,' Mary said again. 'We're practically neighbours.'

'I just thought I'd bring Victoria out to meet a few of the locals,' Lily said, as Victoria sat down at a table and picked up a menu card.

'And I ... have a request,' Victoria said.

'Oh, sure, what can I get you?'

'Ah, an autumn special, if you're still serving them.'

'December's not until next week. With maple and whipped cream? And walnuts on top?'

Victoria gave a nervous chuckle. 'Sounds perfect.'

'Two,' Lily said.

Mary laughed. 'To hell with it. Three. If you don't mind me joining you? I mean, I don't want to be like a weird fangirl or anything....'

Victoria smiled. 'It's quite all right. Um, Lily here has managed to convince me that my books meant a little to some people.'

'A *little* to *some* people?' Mary said. 'They mean a lot to practically everyone I know.'

Victoria gave another little laugh, and Lily grinned. It had taken some convincing to get Victoria out of her new house, but she was becoming more comfortable as the minutes passed.

'Your compliments are very flattering,' Victoria said.

'Don't worry,' Mary added. 'I won't tell a soul. Not unless you want me to.'

'Lily said I could trust you,' Victoria said. 'Which is why I … ah, have another favour, if you don't mind.'

'What, me?'

Victoria leaned down and opened the satchel she had brought. She lifted a thick cardboard envelope and put it on the table.

'It's my next book,' she said, with a shy smile. 'It took a little longer to finish than I'd hoped, but I would be very happy if you could do me the pleasure of reading it, and then letting me know what you think. Kind of a beta reader, so to speak.'

Mary wiped her brow. 'My goodness, I think I'm about to go into labour.'

Lily stood up quickly. 'Seriously?'

Mary shook her head. 'No. It was a pregnant woman's figure of speech. Victoria, it would be an absolute pleasure to read your book. I gather it's a total secret?'

'For now,' Victoria said. 'Thank you very much.'

Lily helped Mary bring over the coffees—although buried beneath mounds of whipped cream, nuts, and maple syrup, it was difficult to be sure what exactly was underneath—then the three of them sat down, and within a couple of minutes they were talking as though they'd all been friends for years.

'So what do you think about Willow River?' Mary asked, nodding at the window. Across the road, skeletal trees encircled the churchyard. Rain blown under the awning by the wind spotted the glass. 'It can get pretty grim over the winter.'

Victoria spooned a lump of cream into her mouth, licked her lips, and lifted an eyebrow.

'I think it's a delightful little place,' she said.

'It'll be a bit weird living with Mother again after all these years,' Michael said, one arm behind Lily's back as they half sat, half lay on the sofa in her parents' living room. Both Pete and Sarah were out, giving them a little space. 'She'll need me for a while until she's properly moved in, but perhaps then I'll look at renting a flat in Brentwell for a while.'

Lily looked at him. 'Really?'

Michael shrugged. 'I mean, I'm a modern man and all that, and I know you're a modern girl, and neither of us believe in whirlwind romances or love at first sight and all those crazy storybook things, but you know, I kind of don't want to be any further away from you than I have to be.'

'What about your work?'

'Well, it's kind of the closed season now, so if you can get a bit of time off work, we can go together. There are so many naff museums I need to show you. You have no idea.'

'I wouldn't miss it for the world,' Lily said. 'Uncle Gus has agreed to sell me the annexe, so I can turn it into a café, but I won't get started until after Christmas.' She leaned into his chest, listening to his heartbeat, feeling the warmth of his body. 'Do you think Victoria's book will be a success?' she asked at last.

'She's only just shown it to her editor and apparently a bidding war for the film rights has started already,' he said.

'That's great. What's your favourite bit?'

Michael leaned sideways and lifted an unkempt stack of printed sheets of A4 paper. He turned over the title page and put the rest on his lap.

'Probably this bit,' he said. 'The dedication.'

He lifted up the page and tilted it towards her. Lily had seen it before, but it still made her smile.

For:
Tiffany
Rebecca
Mandy
Felicity
Penelope
Belinda
and Marigold
The girl who saved everything

'But I have another favourite bit,' Michael said. He flicked through the pages until he found the section that he wanted, near the very back. 'Here,' he said, pointing at a paragraph at the bottom of the page. 'When Lily says to Victoria, "Will you do me the honour of becoming my mother-in-law?" You know, I was just wondering when you were going to say that to mother.'

Lily looked at him. 'What?'

Michael shrugged. 'You know, neither of us believe in all those silly things that I mentioned, like holding a flame for someone you knew in childhood, meeting them by chance, falling in love literally from the first moment their eyes met, having a whirlwind romance, and then getting engaged within a few weeks … but what if we did?' He shifted until their eyes met. 'I mean, I'm not asking you to marry me right now, because your parents' sofa is not really the most romantic of places, particularly with your mother's DVD collection of that terrifying Doreen woman up there on the shelf—I mean, I swear her eyes are following me—but if I found somewhere incredibly romantic, went down on one knee, and held up a ring, what do you think you would say?'

Lily smiled and shrugged, trying to look as casual as possible, when she could be sure her thundering heart was giving her feelings away.

'I suppose,' she said, wishing she could speak in more than a dry croak, 'You'll just have to do it and see.'

Michael nodded. 'Do you fancy a walk down to the river?' he said. 'I'm sure it looks lovely at this time of the year.'

Through the window, the sun was high in a cloudless sky. The last leaves of autumn clung to the tops of the trees, soon to fall.

'I'm sure it does,' Lily said. 'I'm sure it looks lovely.'

'Then, Lily Markham,' Michael said sitting up and turning to face her. 'Would you do me the honour of walking down to Willow River with me?'

Lily nodded. 'Just let me get my coat,' she said.

#####

Acknowledgements

Many thanks goes to Elizabeth Mackey for the cover, Jenny Avery for your endless wisdom, Paige for the editorial stuff, and also to my eternal muses Jenny Twist and John Daulton, whose words of encouragement got me where I am today, nearly ten years after the journey started.

Lastly, but certainly not least, many thanks goes to my wonderful Patreon supporters:

Carl Rod, Rosemary Kenny, Jane Ornelas, Ron, Betty Martin, Gail Beth Le Vine, Anja Peerdeman, Sharon Kenneson, Jennie Brown, Leigh McEwan, Amaranth Dawe, Janet Hodgson, and Katherine Crispin

and to everyone's who's bought me a coffee recently:

Spyke, Lindsay, Rosemary, Mariane, Denise, Janet, Christine, and a couple of anonymous readers

Your support means a great deal. Thank you so much!

For more information:
www.amillionmilesfromanywhere.net